"This Will Be The Last Favor I Ever Ask Of You."

Gillian reminded herself that the pure animal magnetism she felt for him could not overshadow the fact that Bryce was the most infuriating creature God had ever put on this earth. And that she could never forgive him for letting her down when she'd needed him the most.

He cut her to pieces with a look of disdain. "I don't suppose you remember the last favor I asked of you."

Gillian shrugged her shoulders. "You'll have to refresh my memory."

Instead of honoring her request, he said, "I've got to hand it to you. You've got gall waltzing into my life after all this time, acting like a little girl lost and playing on my sympathies."

"Sympathy isn't a word anyone associates with you."

Dear Reader,

The characters in this book are very dear to my heart. I relate in a very personal way to what they are going through. My husband and I struggled to conceive children and had our fair share of heartache along the way. When the doctor informed me that I was pregnant again, following a life-threatening miscarriage, we were ecstatic. Nineteen years later, we feel deeply blessed to have two healthy, wonderful sons.

Their births were complicated, though, and both were Life Flight-ed out of our rural town to Denver Children's hospital where they fought valiantly with completely unrelated congenital issues. Those days had a profound impact on my life. Not every couple was as fortunate as we were to take our precious babies home.

My Christmas wish for Bryce and Gillian and you, dear friend, is to make every moment count and to take special care of each other and yourselves.

Best,

Cathleen Galitz

CATHLEEN GALITZ

THE MILLIONAIRE'S MIRACLE

Published by Silhouette Books
America's Publisher of Contemporary Romance

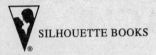

SILHOUETTE BOOKS

ISBN-13: 978-0-373-76823-3
ISBN-10:   0-373-76823-0

THE MILLIONAIRE'S MIRACLE

CATHLEEN GALITZ,

a Wyoming native, teaches English to students in grades 6–12 in a rural school that houses kindergartners and seniors in the same building. She feels blessed to have married a man who is both supportive and patient. When she's not busy writing, teaching or chauffeuring her sons to and from various activities, she can most likely be found indulging in her favorite pastime—reading.

This one is for Mom for showing us how to live with faith, dignity and unwavering love.

One

Gillian Baron formed a fist, lifted it in the air and let it fall to her side—twice—before finally forcing herself to rap on the door of the upscale apartment.

Even then she had to fight the urge to run away like a naughty child, who'd pulled a prank on the neighbors.

Considering that this portal to the past had never been closed to her before, knocking on it now shouldn't feel so surreal.

Maybe he isn't home....

Gillian leaned forward on the balls of her feet and assumed the ready position.

Ready for what? To bolt again? To run away from

all that had once been good and true in her life? Back when life had been as close to perfect as humanly possible and she'd had the key to this man's home—and his heart.

Before everything went so terribly, irreparably wrong.

Before he'd come to hate her.

Sighing in relief at her good fortune to avoid the awkward encounter she'd been dreading, Gillian turned to go.

"I tried," she said, rehearsing what she would tell her sisters when they demanded why she'd failed to speak to him. "Really I tried."

The belated sound of footsteps from inside the apartment caught Gillian midstride.

"I'm coming," rumbled a deep voice.

How she hated being here, dredging up old memories and wallowing in a sea of what once was. Hated dragging Bryce back into the complicated mess that was her life. Hated feeling so terribly vulnerable and weak-kneed after coming to terms with her own solitude at long last.

She doubted he would believe that she was here only on behalf of her father. With typical arrogance, he would more than likely misconstrue her presence on his doorstep as a ploy to finagle a way back into his life. Her pride already sorely tested, Gillian prepared to have the door slammed in her face.

When it finally swung open, Bryce McFadden stood before her in just a pair of faded jeans. His heavy-lidded eyes snapped open in recognition. A flash of something tender streaked across those blue orbs before dark clouds shadowed them and the perfunctory greeting on his lips froze.

"Hell—"

"O?" Gillian finished, hoping that was the intended salutation rather than a deliberate invective. "I hope I didn't wake you."

Seeing him stand at the door half-dressed with his hair bed-tousled and wearing a look of confusion on his unshaven face, she hoped it was just his sleep she'd interrupted and nothing more intimate.

Not that it mattered to her one way or the other.

Still, her stomach rolled as all logic ceased. Dropping her gaze from the silver-blue eyes that were pinning her down, she trained her own on his bare chest, where a mass of curly blond hair dusted its smooth surface. It turned a darker shade just below the sternum before eventually disappearing under the band of his unbuttoned jeans. Heat infused her cheeks when she realized she'd been caught gawking.

Hooking a lazy thumb through a belt loop, Bryce leaned back against the door frame and proceeded to rake her from head to foot with an overtly masculine gaze, with which she was far too familiar. Gillian reminded herself that pure animal magnetism couldn't overshadow the fact that this was the singularly most infuriating creature God ever put on this earth. And that she could never forgive him for letting her down when she'd needed him most.

"May I come in?" she asked, feeling more like the Avon lady than someone with whom he'd once had a life-altering relationship.

"Of course."

As Bryce stepped aside to let her in, Gillian took in his home with a sweeping glance. A big-screen TV, roomy leather couch, matching recliner and exercise equipment saved the place from looking like an efficiency apartment, but the lack of decoration gave it a spartan feel nonetheless. Not a single painting or photograph graced the walls.

Idiot! Did you think he'd keep a photo of you enshrined in his bachelor pad just because you couldn't bring yourself to destroy your own pictures of him?

"Nice place," Gillian said, feigning a nonchalance that matched his own.

She noticed that he hadn't bothered with a Christmas tree this year; a cheerful holiday bouquet on the coffee table was the only acknowledgment that the holiday was only a week away. The arrangement seemed out of place in such masculine digs, but she had to admire his attempt to add color to the austere black-and-white decor that dominated the room. This luxury apartment was nothing like the quaint little Victorian they'd once shared. Squeezing her eyes shut, she fought to forget the images of well-tended flower beds, hand-stenciled accents, antique furniture, a cozy little room decorated with teddy bear wallpaper and—

Stop it!

She couldn't afford to let maudlin memories sidetrack her from the task at hand. Just breathing in and out was proving difficult enough without attempting to battle ghosts at the same time.

"Would you like a cup of coffee?" he asked.

Grateful for anything to keep her hands occupied, Gillian gave him a tight smile.

"That'd be nice."

Bryce helped her shrug off the heavy coat, which was more of a necessity in Cheyenne winters than any kind of fashion statement. The small act of courtesy seemed both familiar and unworldly. In spite of the snow falling outside the window, Gillian felt her temperature rise. Standing in this strange living room inhaling Bryce's familiar musky scent, she could easily recall why she'd loved this man once upon a time. When he left the room to get her coffee, she glanced at the bouquet again, admiring it, and noticed a card sticking out of the blooms. Although Bryce would be back in a minute, she couldn't resist sneaking a peek.

Yes, yes! A thousand times yes!
Love,
Vi

Who the hell was Vi?

Gillian's thoughts turned catty. Had she misread the name? Maybe it was the Roman numeral six and Bryce was into numbering his women now. Or was that hackneyed expression written in feminine scrawl an acceptance of a weekend getaway or something more permanent?

The possibility of Bryce actually asking someone to marry him caused the floor beneath Gillian's feet to undulate. Sternly telling herself that there was too much riding on this meeting to let her imagination get the best of her, she stuck the card back into its little plastic holder before he returned a moment later with two steaming cups of coffee. Her hands shook as she accepted one from him.

"It's instant," he apologized. "Not nearly as good as yours."

Gillian felt a stab of regret that lives once so rich

had been reduced in a single word to the state of a lousy cup of caffeine.

Instant coffee.

Instant messaging.

Instant gratification.

Instant heartache.

"Thanks," she said, taking both the proffered cup and a place on the couch.

She was relieved when Bryce chose a seat in a nearby recliner rather than the empty spot next to her. That way she could speak to him without the risk of physical contact.

Truth be told, it wasn't the current arcing between them that worried Gillian but the deep emotional response this man evoked in her. That Vi's note had the power to send a hot spurt of jealousy coursing through Gillian's veins was disconcerting to say the least.

Taking a sip of coffee, Gillian realized he wasn't lying—it was truly awful. Suddenly she felt inexorably sad to think of him drinking such tepid stuff out of his chipped mug every morning in this sterile place. Especially knowing how much he once savored starting his day with her special brew.

In bed with her.

Setting her cup on the table, she watched Bryce rub the stubble on his jaw. She couldn't help remembering how rough it had felt between the palms of her hands. Not the type to carry on small talk while ignoring the elephant in the room, he looked at her expectantly.

"Why don't I save us both the agony of trying to make small talk?" she offered, searching frantically for the right words to do just that.

"That'd be nice," he drawled.

Bristling at the sarcasm in his voice and unable to think of any way to soft-pedal what she'd come here to say, Gillian simply blurted out the reason for her unannounced visit.

"Stella and Rose want to have Dad declared incompetent."

Launching a grenade in the room would have caused a less appalled reaction on Bryce's face. A muscle twitched in his jaw, and his eyes turned the color of polished gunmetal.

"What's that got to do with me?"

It wasn't exactly the first question Gillian was expecting from him, but it was nonetheless a fair one. Who could blame him for not wanting to be sucked into the drama that was her family all over again?

"By all rights this really isn't your problem," she consented, "but it's not by choice that I'm here."

"Has something happened that I should know about?"

Bryce had always been close to her father, and

Gillian knew his concern was genuine. She struggled to explain the situation without somehow sounding as guilty as she felt. It hadn't been easy pulling her life back together the past two years, but just because her father lived clear across the state and she was keeping limitless hours at work didn't make her feel any better about neglecting the man who had raised her single-handedly after her mother had passed away.

"Stella says he's fallen a couple of times and has been spending money so frivolously and erratically that both of them think he might be suffering from early stages of A-Alzheimer's."

It was hard enough getting the word out of her mouth let alone wrapping her mind around all its awful implications.

Not having actually seen her father since the last holiday when he'd expressed his disappointment in her decision to leave Bryce, Gillian had to rely on her sisters' judgment of his current physical and mental state. And while she couldn't bring herself to believe that either one of them would commit their father to a nursing home just to gain access to his money, she was worried they might be overreacting. Unfortunately their threat to take the matter to court put the onus on her to do something before things got out of hand and irreparable damage was done to the entire family.

· Nothing short of a full-blown emergency would have compelled Gillian to be here otherwise.

Bryce's features softened for an instant. "I'm sorry to hear that."

Sorely tempted to seek comfort in his strong arms as she once would have, Gillian instead focused her attention on a tiny run sneaking up the thigh of her black nylons. Self-consciously tugging at her tweed skirt to hide it, she wondered how, after all the trouble she'd taken to make herself look presentable today, she could have missed such a fashion faux pas. It was the kind of flaw that highlighted her own unraveling state of mind.

She cleared her throat and got down to business. "It turns out that Dad has given both of us equal durable powers of attorney in case he's ever unable to take care of himself."

There was no way Bryce could have faked the shocked look on his face, dispelling once and for all Rose and Stella's notion that he'd personally masterminded this whole thing a long time ago. The harsh words they'd exchanged during the bitter divorce proceedings created a rift Gillian doubted could ever be bridged. Only after the impact of her announcement sunk in did the irony of it register upon Bryce's features.

He coughed up a dry chuckle. "I get it. Your sisters can't commit the old man to the loony bin unless you and I do the dirty work for them."

Unwilling to be drawn into another "discussion" about family dynamics, Gillian tried to keep a defensive note from creeping into her voice.

"Nobody said anything about a 'loony bin.' They have some valid concerns that can't be ignored," she stated coolly. "And there are some lovely facilities in the area."

"Et tu, Brute?"

His words hung in the balance like a tightrope walker stranded in the wind between two opposing fortresses. As much as Gillian resented the Shakespearean implication that she would stab her own father in the back, she was worried that Bryce himself would take a similar view of the legal proceedings her sisters were considering.

Would he be able to separate her from their actions?

More importantly, would she?

Bryce stabbed his fingers through his uncombed hair in exasperation.

"Just what in the hell is it you want from me, Gill?"

Her heart hammered in her chest as she looked straight into those unforgiving eyes of his. And momentarily lost herself there.

"I want you to go to the ranch with me. Dad won't budge from the house until he has a chance to talk to us both together, and my sisters are threatening to initiate proceedings if he doesn't. My father has promised to abide by our joint decision, which is the only way I see of keeping my entire family from falling apart."

Bryce snorted as he dropped his head back onto the cushion of his chair and closed his eyelids. Dark circles hung in half moons beneath them. That he was working too hard came as no surprise to Gillian. She regretted interrupting his sleep on a Sunday morning, but this was the only time she could count on him being home. Besides, as difficult as it was for her to see him, this wasn't a matter she cared to discuss on the phone.

When he finally opened his eyes, Bryce sounded every bit as tired as he looked.

"Suffice it to say I've got a lot going on in my life right now. Why don't I just sign off as executor or whatever the hell it is that John made me, and you and your sisters can divide your thirty pieces of silver however you want?"

Gillian flinched at his words.

"You'd really do that?" she asked, feeling strangely disappointed. Here he was offering to do the very thing for which her sisters were so desperately praying, but while *they* would be delighted with such a decision, this just didn't feel right to Gillian. She was bound more by her own conscience than the rules of a blind and binding legal system.

"I'd do anything to be rid of the Baron clan once

and for all," he snapped. "But I would have thought you at least would have the decency to wait until the old man was dead before laying claim to his estate. You know how much he loves that ranch—and how hurt he'll be by any claim that he's incapable of running it himself."

"You don't think I know that?" Gillian said. The thought of declaring the strongest man she'd ever known to be unfit seemed nothing short of sacrilegious.

"Your father won't take kindly to being caged up in a nursing home," Bryce told her flatly. "He'll never forgive you."

Gillian folded her arms over her chest as if to protect her aching heart and glared at him. "Regardless of what you might think, I'm not any more comfortable with this than you are. If, after seeing him, we're equally satisfied that he's capable of looking after his own affairs, that'll be the end of that. We can both go on with our lives without having to look back on today with regret."

Bryce's harrumph echoed off bare walls.

Fearing that her courage would fail her, Gillian continued on in a rush. "I know it's a lot to ask, but Dad considers you a friend. He trusts you. And despite our past history so do I. Any advice you can offer would be greatly appreciated. Not to mention that you're legally involved whether you want to be or not. As I understand it, I have to agree to your signing off, and I'm not willing to do that until we talk to my father in person and assess the situation ourselves. Considering this could drag on for years if my sisters decide to take the matter to court, it'll be the quickest way to get me out of your life permanently."

Something ugly and hard leaked into her voice as she couldn't resist adding, "I'm sure that's something Vi could appreciate."

Looking surprised that she was familiar with the name, Bryce nonetheless conceded the point.

"Considering that I've asked her to marry me, I'm sure she would."

A seasoned actress couldn't have held herself together any better than Gillian did upon hearing that newsflash. Her chest felt as if it were going to implode, and the difficulty she was having breathing had nothing whatsoever to do with the high altitude.

"Congratulations," she said with difficulty. Hoping not to come off sounding as pitiful or bitter as she felt, she added, "You deserve to be happy. Really."

On some level she really meant it, but her smile hurt.

"I promise this will be the absolute last favor I ever ask of you."

Bryce cut her to pieces with a look of sheer disdain. "I don't suppose you remember the last favor I asked of you."

Gillian gave him a blank look and shrugged her shoulders. "You'll have to refresh my memory."

"It was when I begged you not to divorce me."

Two

"That hardly qualifies as a 'favor,'" Gillian said angrily.

Bryce glowered at her. "No more than the one you're asking of me. I've got to hand it to you, baby. You've got some gall waltzing back into my life after all this time, acting like a little girl lost and playing on my sympathies."

"*Sympathy* isn't a word anyone associates with you," she retorted.

They glared at one another for what seemed forever before Gillian managed to pull herself together.

"I was hoping that you could put aside your

personal animosity for me to do what's best for my dad, a man I happen to know you respect more than your own biological father. A man who trusts you enough to put his fate in your hands—even if you're no longer officially part of the family."

While their father's decision to include Bryce merely annoyed her, it infuriated her sisters. Still, whatever they wanted to believe about Bryce, Gillian knew only John Baron himself was to blame for instigating this awful face-to-face meeting between his youngest daughter and the ex-son-in-law he loved like a son. Gillian hoped her father wasn't playing them all for rubes. God help him if she ever found out he was faking his condition in hopes of contriving a reconciliation between them! The thought filled her with sudden guilt. A *good* daughter wouldn't even entertain such a wicked notion when doctors had confirmed that her father was ill and in need of all the support she could give him.

Hoping a more philosophical approach would better advance her cause, Gillian posed a hypothetical question. "Can we at least agree that fate sometimes brings people together, even when they're doing their best to stay apart?"

"I don't think so."

An exasperated sigh ruffled an errant tendril that

had fallen over her forehead. Clearly she was going to have to appeal to this man's overdeveloped sense of duty if she were to stand any chance of enticing him back to the ranch over the holidays. She knew that severing his relationship with her father had been particularly hard on Bryce. Asking him to become emotionally involved all over again with her crazy family didn't seem fair, especially if her father's condition was truly as dire as her sisters would lead her to believe. Terrified by death's knock at her heart's door, she couldn't imagine anything more painful than watching a disease destroy someone she loved so dearly.

"I'll only admit that I hate leaving John to the mercy of Jekyll and Hyde," Bryce said. "I'm not surprised that they've grown tired of depending on your father's generosity. I'm sure they feel 'entitled' to their inheritance before he squanders it all away on something as unimportant as the ranch he's spent his entire life building."

Gillian bristled at the insult to her sisters. However, since it was a step up from what he used to call them—the "bitch brigade"—she let it pass.

"How I would love to return a measure of the misery those two caused me over the years. I wonder how they'd manage if they were suddenly cut off without a penny?" A smile played with the corners of Bryce's mouth as he mulled over the idea of karmic payback in his head.

Clearly he'd never forgiven them for encouraging Gillian to file for divorce when he could have used their support. Gillian's voice turned as cold as the sleet building up on his front window. "If you could just let go of your anger toward them for one second and focus on a less vindictive—"

Rolling his shoulders as if to shake off the heavy burden that had been placed there, Bryce interrupted, "You always did have a blind spot where Rose and Stella were concerned, and while it shouldn't make a damned bit of difference to me whether those two bitter old maids lock your father away or bamboozle you out of your rightful inheritance, I still consider myself a man of principle. Right is right, and wrong is wrong. So, as much as I resent it, if John has placed his trust in me, I won't let him down."

Gillian's heart stumbled over itself.

"You'll do it?" she asked, wanting to make sure she hadn't misunderstood.

Bryce spelled it out for her in no uncertain terms. "I'll do it for your father. Not out of any sense of misguided sentimentality or obligation to you."

There was little chance Gillian would get the wrong idea about his motives, not when he was looking at her as if she'd just slithered out from under a rock. Biting her lower lip to stop herself from saying what she really thought, Gillian simply nodded.

"Whatever your reasons, I appreciate it," she said. "Thank you."

Those two little words cost her dearly. They hung in the thick space between them as their cups of coffee grew cold and the pendulum of the chrome clock on the wall swung back and forth in a perfect rhythm belying the chaotic nature of life.

Having made up his mind, Bryce suddenly became all business. "How do you propose we coordinate this little adventure?" he asked. "It shouldn't be any problem for me to take time off work over the holidays, but I'd love to get this over with and be home in time for Christmas next week. How about you?"

The eyebrow Gillian raised in disbelief plunged them back into the same old argument that had plagued their marriage.

"I told you I'd eventually be able to spend less time at the office. If only you could have been a little more patient—"

"Patient!" she exploded. "What you called temporary was literally a lifetime."

Apparently unfazed by the intensity of her emotions, Bryce had the acumen to point out the facts coldly. "You weren't the only one who suffered over the course of our marriage. Why are you so certain that your feelings are so much more heartfelt than mine? Do all women assume they have cornered the market on emotion? Or just you?"

Gillian clenched her fists at her sides and wondered how they'd managed to live together as husband and wife for as long as they had without killing each other. At the moment there was nothing she would have loved more than to slap the smug expression right off his face.

"Can we get back on track?" she asked, wanting to appear the more mature of the two. "It's pointless rehashing things we can't change."

She remembered all too well the times she'd complained about him spending so much time on his career to the exclusion of their home life. As a newlywed she'd been stunned by how lonely she'd felt when he was at work. It wasn't as if his hours hadn't been bad before they were married, but a part of her had hoped he'd make her a priority once they'd said "I do." Since the divorce two years ago, however, Gillian had gained new empathy for what it took to make a living. It hadn't been easy earning her real estate license and trying to carve out a niche in a challenging market.

How ironic it was that since becoming a full-time working woman, she'd adopted Bryce's own over-the-top work ethic. Looking back, she wondered if she'd been too hard on him about investing so much energy into his fledgling software business, not that it excused him from neglecting his obligations to his family. It wasn't the need for money nearly as much as his masculine pride and driving sense of ambition that ultimately put such a wedge between them. After all, her father had been more than willing to help them out financially.

"Christmas is a slow time for selling houses," Gillian said, shoving to the back of her mind all the reshuffling she would have to do to keep her broker and clients happy. "Taking a couple of weeks off shouldn't be too difficult," she lied.

It was Bryce's turn to look surprised. "I'm impressed that you've managed to strike the perfect balance between your personal and professional life in such a short time. Or is it safe to assume that your daddy's money is supporting your little foray into the business world?"

"Go to hell." Gillian resented the implication that she was just dabbling in real estate as a hobby courtesy of her father's generosity.

"I've paid every penny back I've ever borrowed from my father—just like you did," she said, taking perverse pleasure in reminding him that he'd once been financially in debt to John Baron, too.

Bryce barely reacted to that jab. While they'd

been married, he'd taken his responsibility as bread winner seriously—much too seriously in Gillian's opinion. It had cost his ego greatly to finally accept help from his father-in-law at her persistent urging. She believed they would have been far better off if her stubborn husband had relied more on family rather than trying to do everything on his own.

"Glad to hear it," he said.

The lopsided grin he gave her had Gillian self-consciously smoothing out a wrinkle in her skirt. She hated to think she was still susceptible to his charms, but wasn't going to make eye contact just in case.

"Sometimes it's hard for me to remember that all you once wanted to be was a wife and a mother."

Gillian was surprised at the unexpected tenderness in his voice. It was true. Had fate not sent her blindly down such a cruel path, she probably would have still been deliriously happy with that humble dream. Struggling to overcome the pain that Bryce's simple observation evoked, she abruptly changed the subject.

"It's sure to be a challenge getting to the ranch this time of year. Flying out of Cheyenne to Jackson Hole shouldn't be much of a problem—except for the exorbitant holiday price they're sure to charge."

Mentally, Gillian clicked off the days remaining until Christmas. Eight total.

"The hard part will be getting from the airport to the ranch in the dead of winter," she added.

Since ten-foot snowdrifts made regular transportation impossible in the winter, Bryce suggested hiring a private helicopter or renting a snow coach.

"It would be easier just to pack in," she countered with the glib attitude of someone raised in the heart of some of the most challenging terrain in the country. "If you don't have any objections, I'll go ahead and make arrangements for Sid to have a couple of snowmobiles ready for us when we get to Jackson."

She wasn't surprised that the thought of strapping himself to a sleek six-hundred pounds of raw power appealed to Bryce's adventurous nature.

When he readily agreed, she asked, "Do you mind if I make a couple of phone calls before I leave to get the ball rolling? The battery on my cell phone died on my way here."

"I think I left the portable phone in my bedroom. It's down the hall and to the right."

Gillian headed in the direction he pointed. A moment later she stood transfixed and trembling in the doorway of his bedroom.

Hearing her gasp, Bryce rushed to her side. "What's wrong?"

Understanding dawned as he followed her gaze to ' the only picture in the apartment. Hanging above his bed the photo of an infant's foot was enlarged many times over so one could truly appreciate the proportions represented within its gild frame. Two thumbs—Bryce's and Gillian's—cradled and dwarfed the tiny foot. A diamond wedding ring glinted in the background.

The photograph had been taken shortly after Bonnie's premature birth, just a few short months before their daughter died of SIDS—while Bryce was at work.

Gillian stepped over the threshold and robotically made her way across the room to stand before the haunting representation of the fragility of life. On the bottom of the frame was a brass plaque upon which a single word was engraved.

Forever.

Bryce reached out to catch her as she stumbled.

Three

Steadying herself, Gillian shrugged off Bryce's helping hand. She'd never fainted before and wasn't about to start now, however shocked she might be. Righteous anger was as good as a shot of adrenaline for shoring up her rubbery muscles.

"What are you doing with that?" she demanded, pointing at the offending image.

The concern in Bryce's eyes vanished so quickly that it made Gillian wonder if she hadn't imagined it there in the first place.

"I'm so sorry," he drawled sarcastically. "I didn't

realize that I needed to check with you before hanging anything on my walls."

Reality trickled in with the light through the window, casting a supernatural glow on the photograph above his bed. She and Bryce were no longer husband and wife, and as such, Gillian had no business judging either his decorating decisions or his emotions.

"I would think such a poignant reminder would render you incapable of getting out of bed every day," she said, her tone wavering between an apology and an accusation.

"Such a poignant reminder of what a lousy husband and father I was, you mean," Bryce paraphrased.

Gillian's silence spoke for itself.

"Then I guess it's a good thing I was a stellar son-in-law," he added caustically. "Otherwise we'd be happily going our own ways like other divorced couples instead of dealing with complicated family matters that shouldn't involve me."

Gillian wouldn't be goaded into admitting how hurt she'd initially been by the discovery that her ex-husband was the co-executor of her father's estate. Choosing water over blood was a blatant betrayal on John Baron's part, especially considering that Bryce was no longer even tied to the family by marriage.

Her gaze drifted back to the touching image on the wall. She'd almost forgotten how tiny Bonnie had been. Swamped by an unstoppable wave of grief, Gillian regretted letting herself be coerced into coming to Bryce's apartment. Just as she had been afraid it would, this encounter only served to stir up painful memories.

Bryce's features softened. "Would you like me to have a copy made for you?" he asked.

Gillian was surprised by his thoughtfulness. For a fleeting instant, she seriously considered the offer. Certainly her own bare apartment could stand such a loving touch. Since moving in, she'd done little but use it as a place to eat and fall asleep after pouring all her energies into long days at the office. Meeting clients at all hours and strong sales were rapidly making her a rising star in her profession and giving her virtually no time to remember her old life. Which was, of course, the point.

"I don't think I could bear it," she explained, amazed that he could.

After Bonnie's death, he had been the one to encourage her to let go of the past and move on. Despite her needing him, Bryce had spent more and more time at work. Although a part of her had wanted to mend their marriage somehow, Gillian's sisters had made her realize that Bryce would never change.

When she presented the divorce papers, he refused at first, but eventually signed. Considering him cold-hearted for putting work ahead of her and Bonnie, Gillian was amazed now to see him immortalize their baby in such a sentimental, moving manner.

Swiping at her eyes with the back of her hand, she struggled to keep from crying. She blinked hard and forced herself to look away. The last thing she could afford to do was think Bryce had changed. A part of her still loved him despite their turbulent past, and she knew herself well enough that any weakness on her part could send her back to his arms.

Damn it!

Bryce had never wanted to make this woman cry, especially when her tears were like kryptonite to him. His reaction astonished him. In spite of all the painful things they'd gone through, he still felt a tug of protectiveness at the sight of her fighting back tears. He'd always had a soft spot where Gillian was concerned.

She was still just as beautiful as he remembered with her Snow White fair complexion, dark hair, amethyst eyes and those full, pouty lips that made all men thank God for making women. There was no denying that lust was what had initially attracted him to her, but that hadn't been the only element at play. The first time they met, he'd felt an aura of goodness surrounding Gillian that one often associated with fairy-tale heroines.

Bitterly Bryce reminded himself that real life didn't promise any magical happily-ever-afters, and that sometimes evil stepsisters triumphed over Prince Charming with poisoned words, not apples. By the time he finally signed the divorce papers with which he'd been served, he couldn't be sure whether Gillian wasn't a monster herself.

She'd averted her gaze from the picture of Bonnie to a photograph on his nightstand. In it, he had an arm draped affectionately around the shoulders of a pretty blonde who was in her mid-thirties. A little tow-headed boy standing next to him clutched Bryce's free hand and grinned into the camera.

"I presume that's Vi." Gillian's voice was flat and devoid of emotion.

Bryce nodded. "And her little boy, Robbie."

"He's adorable."

"He's a great kid."

Bryce went on to explain that in spite of losing his father in a tragic automobile accident, Robbie was an incredibly well-adjusted child, who desperately needed a father. Wanting more than anything to be an integral part of a loving family again, Bryce was ready and willing to step into that role. He felt no need to justify his decision to put his miserable divorce behind him finally and rejoin the land of the living.

"Vi's wonderful, too," he added.

Gillian gave him a wobbly little smile. "I just hope she understands why you're taking off over the holidays to help me."

Bryce steeled himself against the wounded look that smile failed to hide. As a red-blooded American male fired by the memory of making glorious love to this woman, he may have little control over the testosterone rushing through his veins, but he did have a good deal to say about committing to someone who'd once used his heart as a toothpick. He definitely needed to think about Vi's feelings and forced himself to concentrate on the logistics of this trip rather than the scent of the perfume wrapping around him in deceptively strong silken threads.

She had no right to begrudge him any measure of the comfort Vi brought to his life. Or the joy that her little boy shone into his lonely days.

"How soon can you book an available flight?" he wanted to know. "I'd like to get this over with as quickly as possible so I don't miss the look on Robbie's face when he opens his presents."

Bryce felt bad when Gillian's eyes clouded over with longing for all the Christmases they'd never have with Bonnie. To be kind, he neglected to add that he didn't want to miss Vi's response, either, when she unwrapped her present from him: a three-carat diamond engagement ring that was far more impressive than the one he'd barely been able to afford for Gillian once upon a time.

Back when he'd been struggling to make a go of his fledgling company, his starry-eyed bride had assured him she didn't care about the finer things in life like diamonds and fancy trips that he was so bent on buying for her. All Gillian wanted was for him to spend more time at home with her and the baby. Even now, Bryce wished there was some way he could have made her understand about a man's sense of pride. About his need to provide more than just the basic necessities for his family. About his desire to make something of himself that would make a wife proud.

Now that the company he'd started was about to turn his dream of becoming a millionaire into reality, Bryce wondered if Gillian would ever regret leaving him. Since she hadn't believed in him back when it meant so very much to him, he felt that crowing about his success now would be little more than a hollow victory.

Studying the emotions playing across his ex-wife's face, he hoped that Gillian wasn't going to try to make him feel guilty about moving on with his life, especially since he'd never wanted the divorce in the first place. But now that their marriage was over and he had finally come to terms with it, he resented her showing up on his doorstep unannounced, reminding him all over again how very much he'd once loved her.

"I'm happy for you," Gillian said sincerely.

While trying to say the right thing—or at least not the wrong thing—she prayed that the smile pasted on her face didn't look as strained as it felt.

She couldn't imagine anything worse than having to spend time with her ex-husband on a long, drawn-out trip down memory lane while he was in the process of planning his wedding. No matter what the emotional cost, Gillian vowed never to let Bryce know just how much power he still exercised over her battered heart. Nor to interfere in his new life with his picture-perfect, ready-made family.

Upholding her end of a polite conversation wasn't easy, though, when her thoughts kept wandering to his impending nuptials. Would Robbie be the ring bearer or the best man? Would the bride wear traditional white? Would Bryce look as handsome and completely sure of himself as he had on *their* wedding day? Shaking her head as if she could get rid of those unwanted images like an Etch-A-Sketch, Gillian made herself focus on the crisis at hand.

"Are you expecting your parents for the holidays?" she asked, hoping that wouldn't present yet another obstacle to her scheduling nightmare.

Bryce shook his head. "I gave them a cruise for Christmas this year."

"How generous of you," she murmured.

And smart…

Gillian knew the only way his parents would take such a lavish trip would be if someone else paid for it. It came as little surprise to her that his parents would prefer some exotic location to the tedium of decorating a tree, wrapping presents and squeezing in time with a son who never could do enough to please them. Besides, she was no longer around to wait on them hand and foot while Bryce was blissfully off at work. If her sisters were the bane of his life, she could claim the same about his parents. She'd always believed Bryce to be closer to her father than to his own because Sedrick McFadden was so innately selfish. And cheap. The only thing tighter than Sedrick's wallet was his wife's pocketbook, and Gillian was convinced that was because it was welded shut.

She imagined that Bryce's generosity was born of the fear of someday becoming as stingy as them. From the time he was just a kid working both a morning and evening paper route, he'd been expected to earn his keep. Growing up, he'd been on his own much of the time. Only after he married Gillian did Sedrick and Donna decide to make up for lost time by visiting often—always when it was most convenient for them regardless of how busy Bryce was or how exhausted their pregnant daughter-in-law was.

They treated each visit as their gift and her servitude as their just reward. Far more willing to share the good times than the bad with Bryce, they'd given Gillian the distinct impression that it had been a real sacrifice on their part to show up for Bonnie's funeral in lieu of simply sending their regrets.

Pushing aside those stale memories, Gillian tried to make herself present in the moment.

"I'll call you with all the details after I finalize our travel arrangements. I really do appreciate you doing this for me—for Dad, I mean," she amended quickly, feeling her neck redden.

She was growing more desperate by the minute to get out of this stifling place and was grateful when the phone rang, allowing her the opportunity to make a quick getaway. Only after she was safely outside Bryce's apartment did her heart rate start to slow.

Her hands trembled as she punched the buttons on the elevator. Try as she might, it was impossible to get the picture of Robbie's cherubic little face out of her head. She was overwhelmed by old feelings of somehow failing as a woman. They were immediately followed by a swell of bitterness at a God who would give one woman a perfectly healthy child while depriving another of the same joy.

Oddly enough, what cut most deeply wasn't that Bryce was moving on with his life.

With someone else.

And a little blond angel who looked like a custom-ordered replica of Bryce when he was a boy.

It was that, despite severing all ties to her old life, Gillian was permanently mired in the quicksand of the past, watching the rest of the world move on without her.

Four

Three short days later Gillian stood waiting in line at the airport, wondering if Bryce was going to bother showing up at all. Just as she had suspected, it had been a good deal easier obtaining tickets at inflated holiday rates than packing to accommodate the snowmobiles that would transport them on the final leg of their journey. Feeling like Charlie Brown so wrapped up in winter layers that she could barely move, she unzipped her coat to reveal a bulky sweater. Underneath her jeans she wore a pair of pink long johns.

Recognizing her customized ring tone, she

reached for the phone in her coat pocket and flipped it open. Even with all the background noise, Stella's voice was unmistakable. Gillian was relieved that it wasn't Bryce canceling at the last minute.

"No, he's not here yet," she reported.

As irritated as she was at the moment with Bryce, the last thing she wanted to do in a crowded airport was rehash the argument she'd had with her sister earlier about taking Bryce to see their father. Stella couldn't understand why her contrary ex-brother-in-law didn't just gracefully bow out of their private family affairs since he was no longer a member. If she ever found out that Gillian had been the one who actually talked him out of signing off as an executor, there was no telling what kind of protracted family squabble would erupt.

"Still the same old, selfish Bryce, expecting the universe to wait on his overloaded schedule," was her sister's cynical observation.

"He'll be here. Don't worry."

Gillian hoped she sounded more confident than she felt. One could never discount the possibility that Vi had decided at the last minute to keep Bryce at home because she didn't want him alone with his ex. Of course, Vi had nothing to worry about since both Gillian and Bryce hoped they could go their separate ways permanently once they returned.

"Little sister, when are you going to stop counting on men in general and Bryce in particular?" Stella demanded. "I don't understand why you would expect him to take any precious time off from work on such short notice when you're divorced. He certainly didn't bother when you were married, back when it really would have meant something to you."

It still meant something to her, but Gillian wasn't about to admit it. Stella might have good intentions, but her judgmental attitude did tend to grate on her nerves. She wished her sister would spare her the lecture and let her get on with the difficult task at hand. It was hard enough dealing with painful memories without having someone rub salt into old wounds. The strained silence on Gillian's end of the phone did little to discourage Stella. Bryce used to say that she could put a dog with a bone to shame.

"By the way, thanks for the birthday card," Gillian said, hoping to change the subject.

In spite of her sister's faults, she never doubted the sincerity of Stella's concern for her. Still, Gillian was relieved when their conversation was cut short by another call. It came as no surprise that it was from the office. Even though her co-workers had promised to cover for her while she was gone, Gillian was generally considered indispensable at work. Having spoiled her clients with the kind of conscientious, personal attention that was a rare commodity in the business world, it was far more difficult for her to take time off than she'd led Bryce to believe.

It wasn't that her job wasn't gratifying. Aside from the satisfaction of being a financially independent woman, Gillian truly enjoyed matching clients with houses that were perfect for them. She also took special pride in helping young couples purchase their first home; they greatly appreciated the decorating advice she threw in for free. Unfortunately all that talent was wasted on her own minimalist apartment, but Gillian was glad she didn't have to bother asking anybody to water her plants or watch a pet while she was away.

As much as her job served to numb the pain of losing a child and going through a divorce, Gillian was nonetheless ready for a break. It was just too bad that the plane she was boarding wasn't bound for a tropical vacation spot instead of the one place certain to make her feel like a little girl all over again.

"I left all the paperwork for the McVee contract with Becky," she assured her boss before hanging up. Their flighty secretary was certain to be in for a lecture for neglecting to mention the fact to the broker whose blood pressure was dangerously high even on rare days when everything went right at the office.

Stepping up to the boarding gate, she handed the attendant her ticket. "Any chance this flight will be delayed?" she asked, checking her watch for the millionth time.

"There's nothing to indicate that it won't leave according to schedule, but you know what they say about the weather in Wyoming—If you don't like it, just wait fifteen minutes for it to change."

Gillian thought the cheesy saying was just as applicable to Wyoming men as it was to its weather. Casting a final glance over her shoulder, she was relieved to see Bryce racing toward the boarding gate. Her pulse leaped, and she suddenly felt sixteen all over again. Hating the way her fickle body betrayed her, she supposed she should be glad to feel anything at all. For the longest time there had been nothing but pain beneath her skin, and she'd deliberately pushed away anyone who challenged her to feel anything else.

Gillian reminded herself that she had no right to the tingling possessiveness that surged through her veins as every woman in the general vicinity swiveled her head to get a better look at the handsome man who skidded to a stop beside her. She passed him his ticket without saying a word. Instead she gave him one of the aggravated looks she'd perfected in their marriage. That he didn't bother with an explanation—or an apology—only deepened her sense of irritation.

Once on the tiny prop jet, Gillian located her seat next to a window. Since it was far safer concentrating on the tarmac outside than the emotions tearing her up on the inside, she turned to look at a world as bleak as the task that lay before her. Outside, men in jumpsuits cleared ice from the underside of the plane's wings.

"Do you still get nervous about flying?" Bryce asked, sliding into the seat next to her.

She nodded, remembering how he used to hold her hand before the engines even wound up and didn't let go until they were safely in the air.

Feeling like a pebble about to be launched from a slingshot, Gillian told him, "Takeoffs are still the worst."

"Better than bumpy landings."

Digging her fingernails into the armrests, she wondered if he was referring to one that lay ahead of or behind them.

"Welcome aboard, ladies and gentlemen," a masculine voice announced over the intercom. "Today we'll be cruising at an altitude of twenty-six thousand feet. At the present time the weather in Jackson Hole is a chilly twelve degrees. Due to our short flight time, I would request that you keep your seat belts fastened until we arrive."

The fact that she was wrapped up like a Christmas

present made little difference to Gillian when Bryce's hand settled on her thigh after he reached over to fasten his seat belt. Even through layers of clothing, his touch had the power to make her flinch. Hoping he hadn't noticed, she didn't release her death grip on the armrest until she heard the landing gear retract.

"Thanks," she muttered.

"No problem." He grinned, making her wonder if she was the only one who felt the charge between them.

Determined not to dwell on it, she folded her hands demurely in her lap to hide their telltale tremors and studied the landscape below.

Intricate patterns of snow fences snaked across the Great Plains for miles in all directions. From this vantage point she thought she and Bryce may have just as well been crossing the arctic tundra of Alaska as the frozen prairie of Wyoming. It was hard to imagine the hardships that men like her great-grandfather had to endure in laying claim to this land through homestead laws intended to settle the rugged West.

When Bryce struck up a friendly conversation with another passenger, Gillian found herself resenting how much more easily he could talk to complete strangers than to her. By the end of their marriage it seemed they could barely manage to mumble simple courtesies to each other let alone hold real, meaningful conversations. Just as she feared when she first decided to contact Bryce, all the old horrible feelings associated with their divorce came tumbling back.

Gillian dreaded returning to the solitude of wide-open spaces where there was no way of ignoring the ghostly voices of the past echoing off the red canyon walls, but she was no longer so certain that running away was the best way to rebuild a shattered life. Studying the lay of the land with a bird's eye perspective, she couldn't help but wonder if she might have been happier had she stayed put rather than succumbing to the allure of geographical change.

When the Grand Tetons loomed into view, looking more like the Swiss Alps than anything belonging in North America, Bryce asked her permission to get a better look.

"By all means."

She instantly regretted those words.

The warmth of his breath against her cheek when he leaned across her seat was enough to make her light-headed. The smell of his favorite cinnamon gum took her back to a time when she'd felt free to kiss him whenever the urge took her—as it did now. She beat back that urge with a vengeance.

"Does your father have any idea how much the old homestead's gone up in value over the years?" Bryce asked, apparently unaffected by their close proximity.

"I doubt it."

Gillian didn't really want to talk about market values. It saddened her to think about selling the home where she'd grown up. No matter how much profit was involved, some things just couldn't be measured in dollars and cents.

From fifteen thousand feet up she was surprised to see Jackson Hole encroaching upon the wilderness that abutted the snowy valley lying at the foot of those majestic mountains. One fabulous mansion after another was being built in what was quickly becoming the Beverly Hills of the West. Perhaps it was too much to ask that the quaint mountain town of her childhood remain the same when she herself had undergone so many changes.

"With so many millionaires having two or three trophy homes, I wouldn't be surprised if most of those sprawling estates are vacant during the winter except for an occasional ski weekend or holiday," she offered in the way of polite conversation.

"I'd bet every cent of your next commission that both of your sisters know exactly how much the land is worth."

Gillian threw up her hands to ward off the attack. "Can't we just leave them out of this?"

"I would love nothing more than to leave them out of the rest of my life," Bryce rejoined, "but I have a sneaky suspicion they aren't about to let that happen any more than they could keep their noses out of our business when we were married."

"Why is it so hard for you to believe that they're as torn up about this as I am?" Gillian snapped, rushing as she always did to her sisters' defense.

"Maybe because you love that old man as much as I do. Or at least you once did."

Gillian felt her blood pressure soar. The man could provoke a saint to violence.

"Who are you to question my loyalty—"

Her response to his provocations was interrupted midsentence as they hit an air pocket and Gillian's stomach lurched into her throat.

The pilot's voice crackled over the intercom. "We're experiencing some turbulence and ask that you stow all unsecured items under the seats or in the overhead bins. Please fasten your seat belts and put your seat backs in the upright position."

Gillian hoped it was nothing serious. She had no desire to spill her guts to her ex-husband as her life flashed before her eyes and their plane crashed into the white abyss below. Still, when Bryce wrapped an arm reassuringly around her shoulder, she didn't pull away. Grateful to have something warm to hold on to, she knew better than to read anything more into the gesture than kindness inspired by the terrified expression on her face. Even so, a comforting squeeze flooded her mind with memories of intimate moments they once shared.

Looking at that big masculine hand on her shoulder, she remembered the simple gold wedding band she'd given him. Inside, she'd inscribed it with the same naive word that blindsided Gillian when she'd discovered it below that incredibly moving photograph in Bryce's bedroom.

Forever.

"Trust me," Bryce said in a voice that somehow managed to sound more authoritative than the captain's. "Everything's fine."

Gillian desperately wanted to believe him—just as she had when they'd made their vows to one another. Those words came back to her as clearly as the day they said them to each other in front of a crowded church.

In sickness and in health.

Until death do us part...

As the plane bounced through another air pocket, a collective groan filled the cabin. Gillian sought strength in Bryce's calm demeanor and steady gaze. Those eyes had seen their fair share of dreams both fulfilled and shattered without losing their shine.

"Hold on," Bryce said, wrapping his arms around her and pressing her tightly against his chest.

Gillian felt the strong beating of his heart against hers as they hit the runway.

Hard.

As the sound of brakes roared in her ears, she squeezed her eyes shut. The first thing she saw when she finally opened them was an amused expression on Bryce's face as the plane rolled to a safe, anticlimactic stop.

"How are you doing?" he asked.

Gillian hadn't seen such tenderness in his features for a long, long time. It was her undoing. Tears welled up in her eyes as she somehow managed a squeaky "fine" in response.

Fine. Except that being with you scares me more than the thought of hitting the ground at two hundred miles per hour....

Gillian told herself that it was ridiculous to get sucked back into any fantasy that involved reviving a dead relationship. A little turbulence shouldn't make her forget that not only were they divorced but that Bryce was engaged to another woman. One she assumed could give him even more children than the healthy little boy whom he already adored.

As the captain announced their safe arrival, Gillian struggled to regain a sense of composure. In the seat in front of her a young mother was busily reassuring her four-year-old that everything was all right. She wiped away the tears rolling down the girl's chubby little cheeks and gathered her into her arms.

Gillian's own arms ached at the sight.

"There's nothing to be afraid of, honey," the woman promised. "We're safe and sound on the ground now, and Daddy's waiting to take us home."

The toddler took solace in the thumb she stuck into her mouth and studied Gillian solemnly over her mother's shoulder. That she would have been a wonderful mother herself was of little consequence in the flickering shadows of dead dreams. Stepping off the plane into a subzero blast of air did nothing to lift the sense of depression that settled into Gillian's heart. Against the imposing background of the Tetons, the wind whistling through the valley was bitter and merciless. The dark bank of clouds building up in the distance predicted even colder weather to come.

In the short walk from the plane to the terminal, she felt the sting of the cold against her exposed face. She wasn't looking forward to traveling in such frigid weather. Making her way inside the airport, she welcomed the miracle of central heat. Since neither Bryce nor she had brought along more than carry-on baggage, there was little to do but wait for a taxi to take them to Sid's Outpost, where an old friend would outfit them with snowmobiles and all the latest gossip.

They'd barely pulled out of the airport before Bryce was on the phone to Vi. It wasn't so much his conversation as the loving tone with which he conveyed the routine details that made Gillian wish she could crawl out of the back of the taxi.

"I miss you, too," he said a moment later. "I'll call as soon as we get to the ranch so you don't worry."

Gillian heard him chuckle deeply.

"Robbie said that? What did the teacher say?"

He paused for her reply and then laughed again.

"Would you mind putting him on the phone? I'd really like to talk to him."

The loving expression on Bryce's face left little doubt that he had truly bonded to the boy. Gillian's stomach roiled as she pictured the two of them together doing all the things a father and son should. All the things he would never get to do with Bonnie.

"Hey, slugger, how're you doing? Your mom tells me you've been helping her wrap presents. I'm going to do my best to get back in time for Christmas. You stay off Santa's naughty list, and I'll be home before you know it. I'm also going to try to get a couple of tickets for that Nuggets game in Denver that we've been talking about."

Bryce probably would have chatted longer had the cell service in the mountains not been so spotty. Before saying his final goodbye, he told Robbie to "take good care of your mother. It's important to look out for those you love—no matter how old you are."

Gillian bristled at the implied censure she imagined to be directed at her.

"You have no right to judge me," she said as he put his phone away. "I don't need you to make me feel any guiltier than I already do."

"Who said I was judging you?" Bryce asked.

"Right!" she intoned sarcastically. Gillian didn't buy his innocent act for an instant.

Although the heater in the taxi was on full blast, it did little but push the cold air to the back of the vehicle. There was certainly no chance of it thawing the chill building up between the two passengers who would rather look out their respective windows than risk speaking to each other again. Gillian blew on her hands and rubbed a hole in the frost-covered window. An eagle flew across her line of sight. Farther down the road a bullet hole added unnecessary punctuation to a No Hunting sign posted on a buckboard fence.

Such familiar sights brought back memories of the times she'd spent riding the range with her father. He was the one who instilled in her an abiding love of nature. As miles passed without a word being spoken, they neared the town of Kelly, a community so small it barely warranted a dot on the map.

Bryce was the first to break the silence. "When we get to the ranch, do you think we could pretend this isn't as painful as it really is—if only for your father's sake?"

"Only if you can stop trying to make me feel like such a terrible daughter every chance you get."

"That's your conscience talking, not me."

It wasn't because Gillian found that nasty dig unworthy of a reply that she clamped her mouth shut and refused to dignify it with a response. But rather because, deep down inside, she suspected he was right.

Five

Some things never changed.

Gillian counted herself lucky that Sid Meridan was one of them. His grizzled features and rough manner were as famous around these parts as the bottomless cup of coffee featured on his limited menu. A person could spend hours catching up over one of those white cups feeling right at home. An unlikely looking Good Samaritan, Sid had been a fixture in Kelly for as long as Gillian could remember. His Outpost was a restaurant, gas station, snowmobile rental and sales office and community gathering hole.

Years ago he'd sold Gillian's father one of the first Kitty Cats ever made and had taught her how to drive the child-size snowmobile. He'd also been there to pull her out of a ditch when she'd had her first car accident. At seventeen she'd swerved to avoid a moose that had lumbered out of the woods in front of her one snowy evening. Sid had placed the call to her father and had assured him that his youngest daughter was safe and sound. He'd also been a pallbearer at her mother's funeral.

"How the hell have you been?" Sid asked, pumping their hands simultaneously.

A wide smile revealed that he'd lost yet another tooth. Soon they were exchanging pleasantries about Gillian's father, the anticipated length of their stay, snow conditions and the weather forecast, as well as the perplexing state of the world in general.

"I've got two machines serviced and ready to go for you," he told them. "John's made arrangements to pay for whatever you need in the way of clothing, helmets and boots so go ahead and pick out whatever suits your fancy."

"I hope your sisters don't take your father's generosity as another sign the old man's lost his mind," Bryce said.

Gillian struggled to maintain a polite smile if only for Sid's sake. A headache had settled in behind her right eye, and the thought of airing personal business in public didn't do much to lessen it. Swallowing the acrimonious response on the tip of her tongue, she headed for the nearest rack of snowmobiling attire. While she sorted through various styles and sizes, Bryce wandered over to look at the latest sled gleaming on the showroom floor. He'd always had a weakness for fast machines whether they were cars, jet skis or snowmobiles. With all the gadgets and the creature comforts available, combined with 185 horsepower, the model that captured his attention sported an eye-popping sales tag.

"SPP included," Sid said with a knowing wink.

Bryce chuckled at the local reference to the "small penis package" designed for egomaniacs who had more money than brains.

"In the old days, this baby'd be sitting here a good long time before anybody'd be willing to pay the sticker price," Sid explained. "Now I have trouble keeping 'em in stock."

While Gillian slipped into a changing booth to try on her bibs and matching coat, Sid filled Bryce in on the monumental changes affecting the valley.

"Traditional working ranches are selling for millions and being repackaged as 'ranchettes.'"

He gave the word as much respect as the wad of chew rolling around in his mouth. "I've heard rumblings that some big-time developer's been speculating about dividing up Moon Cussers, as well."

A muscle in Bryce's jaw vibrated. "Do you think John knows anything about it?"

"Doubt it."

The name of his ex-father-in-law's ranch evoked images of pirates rather than cowboys since, in days of old, the term was associated with scoundrels living near the New England coast who deliberately hung false lights out so that captains would mistake them for beacons and run their ships aground, allowing the brigands to pillage the disabled vessels. They cursed the moon because its glow would reveal their scheme to crews of passing ships.

A curious transplant from Maine, John's great-grandfather established himself as a respected cattle baron only after getting his start in the business by rustling mavericks from other herds. He, too, was rumored to swear at the moon on nights when there were no clouds to hide his activities from law-abiding cattlemen. Of course, none of this had ever been proven beyond local lore.

After indulging in a steaming cup of coffee and a cinnamon roll so huge it spilled over the edges of their respective plates, Gillian and Bryce set out for the ranch dressed more like a couple of explorers ready to conquer the North Pole than modern-day voyagers. Eighteen miles wasn't that long a distance, but Gillian knew such a venture could easily take thirty minutes to two hours depending on conditions. Sometimes inclement weather made the trip altogether impossible.

It had been a long time since she'd been on a snowmobile, and she enjoyed the feeling of being out in the wide-open spaces again. Her sisters could barely contain their contempt for such an inconvenient mode of transportation, but she enjoyed the sense of freedom that only a snowmobile could provide. She couldn't remember the last time she'd had such a feeling of power at her fingertips.

Bryce flew past her in a blur, stirring her competitive spirit. She pulled the throttle to the handle bar and held on tight. An instant later she was arching a rainbow of snow in his direction as she shot by him. Waggling the rear end of her snowmobile, she deliberately taunted him. Out of the corner of her eye, she caught a glimpse of his machine edging up beside her.

Fat chance! she thought to herself.

Gillian veered off the groomed trail toward the archway marking the edge of her father's property. Since the ranch abutted one of the largest elk refuges in North America, only an outsider might consider it odd that the arch itself was made of interlocking antlers. Unmarred by a single human track, the snow was a pristine blanket of white. She and Bryce crisscrossed open meadows, played cat and mouse with each other and reveled in a vast playground where there was nothing to catch the wind but an open heart.

A coyote ventured out from a nearby copse of bare aspens to chase a snowshoe hare that would have been impossible to see in its winter coat had it not been moving. Gillian turned her machine to dissect their path, purposely cutting the predator off from its prey. With a startled yip the coyote scurried in the other direction as she brought her sled to a halt.

"That was for Mr. Floppers," she said, recalling a morning many years ago when she'd awakened to the sight of an eagle feasting on her pet bunny outside her bedroom window.

Gillian's chest tightened at the sight of Bryce climbing the side of the mountain with determination written on his face. He looked tiny against the distant timber line. And uncharacteristically vulnerable.

At the top of his ascent, the snow began to give way like sugar. Any amusement Gillian might feel about his need to show off for her was overshadowed by the thought of him rolling that big machine down the mountainside. She shut off her own snowmobile and removed her helmet. When Bryce pulled up next to her a little while later covered in a layer of fine powder, Gillian couldn't help but feel relief that he was still in one piece.

He took his helmet off to reveal eyes the same color as the sky overhead. They were shining with exhilaration. Gillian squinted against the waning light. Bryce looked exactly like the young man she'd fallen in love with years ago.

"You've got something in your eye," he said, pulling off a glove and reaching out to remove a fat snowflake from the tip of her eyelashes.

When he trailed his index finger down the side of her face, Gillian's corresponding shiver went far beyond anything that the cold could induce.

"We'd better get going. I don't like the looks of those clouds in the distance," she said, replacing her helmet on her head.

The ominous rumbling they heard had nothing to do with the clouds, however. Such bitter cold weather didn't breed thunderstorms in the dead of winter. Only when the windshield on Gillian's snowmobile started vibrating did she grasp the precariousness of their situation.

"Avalanche!" Bryce screamed.

Directly above them a huge cornice broke loose from the cliff face. Careening down the mountainside in what looked like slow motion, the oncoming snow-slide appeared as harmless as a snowball.

Gillian knew better. As it gained speed, that little snowball could very well bring the entire mountain down upon them in less than a couple of minutes.

"Follow me!" Bryce yelled, pointing his machine in the opposite direction and giving it everything it had.

Wrapping her hand around the throttle, Gillian leaned forward as if to urge her machine onto the frozen lake that stretched in front of them. She didn't dare look back as boulders disappeared behind her and trees snapped in two as they vanished beneath a rolling wave of snow that churned up anything that got in its way. It was all she could do to keep ahead of the thunder. The roar drowned out the warning crack of ice beneath her sled. Roosterlike tails of water fanned out behind her runners. In less than five minutes she and Bryce managed to cross the half-frozen lake, which they should have never been on in the first place.

Once safely on the other side and away from imminent danger, Bryce slid to a stop in front of her.

"Gillian!" he cried.

Dropping his helmet into the snow, he attempted to run to her. In three and a half feet of fresh powder that was no easy feat. Sinking to his chest, he crawled toward Gillian on his belly.

The thin line separating love and hate dissolved in a blur of snowy landscape and tears as Gillian pulled off her own helmet, then dropped into the snow and reached out for Bryce. Their fingertips touched, and a moment later they were holding on to each other as tightly as if fate might make yet another attempt to snatch one from the other.

"Are you okay?" Bryce asked.

His words echoed in the deafening silence and lodged in the empty place inside Gillian's heart. She could only reassure him with a nod. It would be a while before words would come.

Anticipation thrummed through her entire being as Bryce lowered his face toward hers. An instant later his lips claimed hers with a ferocity that would have been frightening under any other circumstance. She responded in kind, deepening the kiss by slipping her tongue into the warmth of a sensual mouth that remembered every inch of her body. Closing her eyes, she willingly granted him access to her very soul.

Oblivious to snowflakes falling around them, they devoured one another. A primitive sound emanating from somewhere deep in Bryce's core evoked in her a mewling response that was nearly drowned out by the hammering of her heart. Gillian filled her lungs with the all too familiar scent of his cologne, which she had never been able to forget, no matter how hard she tried.

All of the things that she'd wanted to say to him but had never been able to put into words seemed magically conveyed in the power of that single devastating kiss.

Pulling away from her, Bryce cleared his throat. "I—I don't know why I did that. Um, what do you say we get you home before anything else can go wrong?" he asked with a strained smile.

Home!

Gillian liked the sound of that word. Her residence might be hundreds of miles away, but her real home lay somewhere beyond the next hill.

The question was which one?

As much as she hated to admit that she'd become disoriented by Bryce's kiss, the truth was Gillian had no idea where they were. Any sign of the groomed trail had been completely wiped out by the avalanche, effectively and indefinitely cutting them off from the rest of the world. Even if by some miracle they managed to find their way to the ranch, being near Bryce was every bit as frightening to Gillian as the avalanche itself.

Six

The look on Gillian's face must have told Bryce everything he needed to know about her unraveling state of mind.

"Everything's going to be okay," he promised. "We just got turned around trying to outrun the avalanche. All we have to do is skirt the edge of the lake and keep on going until we make our way back to where the trail used to be. The ranch should only be a couple of miles away from there."

Gillian donned a brave smile. He was right of course. They just needed to stay together and keep their wits about them.

"I'll break a trail for you. Stay in my tracks and keep your speed up so you don't get bogged down," Bryce said.

Gillian was not affronted by the directives. If something were to happen and they became stuck in the snow, it would take an inordinate amount of energy to dig out the machines. And if, for some reason, they couldn't break free, they'd have to spend the night in the middle of nowhere waiting for help to arrive.

"Let's get out of here," Bryce barked.

A little over an hour later, they emerged from a heavily wooded area into an open meadow where Gillian recognized a couple of familiar landmarks. She began to breathe more easily. Cresting a nearby hill soon after, she caught her first glimpse of the ranch and was flooded with love for a place she was convinced was the most special in the world. Through the falling snow, it looked more like a Currier and Ives engraving than an actual home where people lived. A curl of smoke coming out of the chimney reassured her that even if the avalanche had cut off all electricity and telephone service to the house, at least her father was warm and cozy.

She wished she could say the same about herself. No matter how advanced the technology, top-of-the-line equipment and thermal clothing were still no match for prolonged exposure to the piercing cold in this part of the country. She was pretty sure that her hands, which she had wrapped around the heated handlebars, were the only parts of her body that weren't chilled to the bone. Never had Gillian seen a sweeter sight than the Moon Cussers' sign marking the entrance to an estate that had been passed down from one Baron generation to the next. Constructed of ancient logs, the original house qualified for the National Historic Register. Numerous additions over the years remained true to the integrity of the structure and only added to its value and beauty.

Parking their snowmobiles by the hitching rack out front, Gillian was too cold to pay attention to the symbolic clash of past and present. She and Bryce tarried only long enough to drape their helmets on their handlebars before heading for the front door, which swung open before they could reach it.

"I'll be damned!" said the grizzled man who stood waiting for them in the doorway. A wide smile graced his weathered features. "You made it after all. I was just about to call Search and Rescue to go looking for you."

"That might not have been such a bad idea," Bryce said as he stomped the snow off his boots.

John Baron may have shrunken a little since the last time he'd embraced his daughter, but even at a gnarled six foot one he was still a big man with the spare frame of someone who'd worked hard all his life. Gillian's greeting was muffled in his shoulder as he enveloped her in one of his famous bear hugs. He smelled of flannel, pipe tobacco, Old Spice— and home.

"Dad!"

That little word was almost too big to fit through Gillian's throat. Brushing a kiss against the stubble of his cheek, she closed her eyes against the tears welling to the surface. Just stepping through the front door made her feel like daddy's little girl all over again. Safe and sound.

She was sorry that she'd let her own insecurities keep her away for so long. "Come on in. You're letting all the warm air out," he said, ushering them inside.

Gillian watched as he shook hands with Bryce. His father's eyes reflected the sincerity of the welcome as the two renewed their unique bond with the time-honored gesture of respect. In these parts, a firm handshake was still as good as a signed contract.

"You have no idea how much it means to me that you're here," John said. "It just doesn't feel like the holidays without family around."

The comment warmed Gillian in a way that no heater ever could. Frankly she'd been a little worried as to how she might be received. The last time she'd spoken to her father on the phone, they'd fought bitterly. John Baron never bothered hiding the fact that he thought Gillian had made a terrible mistake divorcing the man he considered a son.

"What took you so long?" he wanted to know.

"That's a story that will take some time to do justice to. Do you mind if we have something hot to drink before launching into it?" Bryce asked.

John was anxious to hear all about it. While he went into the other room to fix them a hot toddy, Gillian shed her layers of cold, wet clothing in front of the roaring fireplace. Bryce dug his cell phone out of a zippered pocket and speed dialed his fiancée before he even bothered to take off his boots.

Gillian didn't want to eavesdrop, but he practically had to shout to overcome the static on the line. He walked over to the front window in the hopes of improving the reception.

"Hey, baby, it's me," he said in the breezy way of a man in love. "The good news is that we made it to the ranch all in one piece. The bad news is that it might be awhile until I can get out of here. I hate to tell you this, but there's been an avalanche and I don't know if I'll be able to get back in time for Christmas. I'm sorry."

Gillian felt like taking the phone from him and apologizing to Vi herself as an image of Robbie's disappointed face flashed before her eyes. She really did feel terrible about taking Bryce away from his new family. She couldn't help but notice how careful he was to downplay the most upsetting details about their journey to spare his fiancée any unnecessary worry—details that included a kiss that Gillian could still feel.

"I'll do everything in my power to get home as soon as I can," he promised. "I want to make sure that everything is settled here before we leave John all alone here again. It may take a couple of days before the trail is safe to travel. I wouldn't be surprised if the Forest Service doesn't come in with some dynamite to try to knock the snow loose from the peaks to prevent other avalanches like the one we outran today."

The expression on his face gave no indication that the woman at the other end of the conversation was nothing but *Saint Vi*, Gillian thought.

"I love you, too," Bryce said before disconnecting.

Gillian turned away so he couldn't see what effect those words had upon her. She'd never been the jealous type, but it was hard not to resent the happiness that Bryce had found.

By the time her father returned with three steaming mugs, she was soaking up the heat from the fire and trying to rub some warmth back into her frozen derriere. Certain that Vi would never present herself in such a ridiculous fashion, she was glad that Bryce refrained from making any jokes about her unfeminine long johns.

While he filled John in on the details of their harrowing adventures, Gillian savored her drink. Staring out the front window, she watched as big, wet snowflakes covered the world with nature's lace. In the fading light of shortening winter days, the pine trees cast long shadows across the front yard.

And across her thoughts.

Rolling her cup between her palms, Gillian wondered how she could possibly broach her concerns about her father's well-being without getting him all riled up in the process. Although he'd agreed to talk to Bryce and her about his health, there was no guarantee he wouldn't put up a fight.

"You're lucky you weren't killed," was John's assessment when Bryce had finished the story.

Taking a deep breath, Gillian saw an opportunity to plunge into territory where even angels dared to tread.

"While we're on the subject of dangerous scenarios, it worries me to think about you all alone and cut off from the world," she said. "What if something awful were to happen when nobody was here to help you?"

"Then I'd die a happier man than I would as an invalid in some old folks' home," he said unequivocally.

Ignoring the warning glance her father slanted her

way, she continued. "That won't change the fact that
your family is worried sick about you."

Her father bowed his neck. "Listen here, missy. I
didn't ask you to come here to fret over me. I just
want you and Bryce to help me put some matters to
rest. That's all. Nobody's putting me out to pasture."

Gillian didn't appreciate his scolding tone. Why
should she be made out to be the bad guy just because
she had the audacity to express her concerns? Having
already lost so much, she couldn't bear the thought
of losing her father, as well.

"And don't forget that Dustin's still around," he
added with a huff, referring to the ranch foreman
who lived in a smaller house nearby on the property.
"He and Bette check in on me just about every day."

Gillian was on the verge of saying that every other
day wasn't good enough when Bryce jumped in with
a question she presumed he asked simply to change
the subject.

"How are the Nickelsons doing anyway?"

Although the tension in the room eased as the conversation took a less contentious path, Gillian wasn't
sure she approved. The issue of how much longer her
father could continue to live on his own in such a
remote location would have to be addressed sooner or
later. Bryce might very well think that she was bor-
rowing trouble too readily by bringing it up so soon,

but she'd never been much for putting off the inevitable, no matter how unpleasant it might be. Including filing for divorce so soon after Bonnie's death.

"Dustin and Bette dropped off a Christmas tree just this morning," John said, pointing to a massive blue spruce propped up in a corner of the room. "It's a little more than I'm up to this year so I'm hoping you two don't mind decorating it. It looks like we'll have plenty of time to enjoy it."

It was the first time Gillian had ever heard her father acknowledge any physical limitations, and she felt bad about secretly questioning his motives in bringing the two of them back here. The scent of Christmas in the air took her back to a time when she'd loved the holidays. Since Bonnie's death, she couldn't bring herself to buy a tree let alone decorate one. She'd thought about investing in an artificial tree, a little one that wouldn't demand much from her. Certainly nothing that would require digging through boxes of ornaments for fear of stumbling on any marked "Baby's First Christmas."

She pinned a bright smile on her face and said, "Sure, Dad. That sounds like fun."

"I'll bring the decorations down from the attic tomorrow if that's where you still keep them," Bryce offered.

Trimming a tree was the least they could do for a

man who had done so much for both of them, especially if this proved to be her father's last Christmas at the ranch. Gillian recoiled at the thought. As spry as ever, he looked better than she'd expected. From the way Stella talked, though, death was practically knocking at his door.

Was it possible that her sisters had misjudged his health?

Gillian didn't even want to entertain the possibility that Bryce was right about them exaggerating his condition simply to benefit their own personal agendas. If the chili he served for dinner that night was any indication, his stomach at least was holding up as well as those of men half his age. The food was just as hot and spicy as Gillian remembered. Being home seemed to sharpen all her senses; while she wasn't sure she wanted to awaken her appetite so completely, she didn't have much choice in the matter.

Sitting across the table from her in a pair of form-fitting jeans and a dark turtleneck, Bryce looked even more handsome than she remembered. The lines of experience that once eluded his youthful face had turned him into a ruggedly good-looking man. Gillian knew that most women would line up to offer him what she had once held so dear. An idealistic romantic, she'd asked him to wait until their wedding night to consummate their vows.

And had not been disappointed by what an amazing lover he'd proven to be.

Even if the kiss they shared in the woods was borne out of the relief of surviving a near-death experience, it still had the power to rekindle a passion she'd thought had died long ago. Gillian was afraid that such longings might well stir a blaze that, left untended, would burn with an intensity that knew no bounds—and had the power to destroy everything in its path.

"It's way past my bedtime," her father said, admitting to yet another sign of advancing age.

Gillian glanced at her watch. It was barely eight o'clock. As he struggled to get out of his chair, she cringed to hear his bones creak and was surprised when he headed in the opposite direction of his bedroom.

"I converted the downstairs den into my living quarters last month," he explained, "so I don't have to deal with the stairs. They were getting to be too much for me. You two take the rooms upstairs. Bryce can have mine, and you can sleep in your old room."

Those rooms were right next to each other, and Gillian would have liked a more respectable distance between the two of them for the duration of their stay. She dismissed the temptation to blame the sleeping arrangements on a misguided attempt by a romantic old fool to force a reconciliation between her and Bryce. Clearly, if her father moved downstairs because he was having trouble navigating the stairs, Stella and Rose weren't entirely mistaken in their assessment of his failing health.

When John stumbled suddenly, Gillian felt instant repentance for ever doubting his motives. She jumped to her feet and rushed to his side.

"Let me help you," she insisted.

He accepted her assistance with uncharacteristic meekness. "Did I mention how glad I am you're here?" he asked.

Gillian nodded.

"Me, too." She was a little surprised she meant it. "I'd forgotten how much I missed home."

John smiled. There was less censure than longing in his voice when he added, "There's a lot to be missed around here if you'll just give yourself permission to remember them."

Making their way down the relatively short hallway to a separate section of the house, Gillian couldn't help worrying what would happen should something befall her father out here all alone.

"I'd die a happier man than one locked up in an old folks' home…."

Remembering the conviction in those words, she wondered if there could be a finer gift than allowing someone you love to live life on his own terms. Gillian was relieved to see that her father's quarters were just as nice as the rest of the house. She also noticed that he'd ordered a new recliner, one with a lift kit built in to help him get in and out of it.

An old friend awaited John on his bed. A graying Irish setter lifted his head off the pillow and wagged a tired tail in acknowledgment of Gillian's presence.

"Padre!" She rushed over to embrace the beloved pet that had been part of their family for the better part of two decades.

The old dog barked without getting up and licked Gillian's hand in appreciation at the affection she lavished on him.

"I can remember when he was just a pup," she said, finding it hard to believe he was still with them.

"Poor old guy's just about blind," John told her. "He's losing his teeth, too. In fact, he's not much use around here anymore. Probably not worth that expensive soft food I buy him. I know I should probably put an end to his suffering, but I just can't bring myself to do it."

His voice quivered a little as he added, "I'd like to think somebody would do the same for me when the time comes that I'm no longer good for anything."

Tears sprang to Gillian's eyes. "Don't talk like that," she scolded. "And don't worry about Padre. It's no bother taking care of those we love."

She heard the echo of what Bryce told Robbie on

the phone back in the taxi. Although she shared her father's views on quality of life, she wanted him to understand that there was a good deal more to love than sentimentality alone.

"A person, or a dog's worth for that matter, can't be measured by how productive he is or how much trouble he becomes."

Gillian understood how important it was to protect those she loved from all the practical people who coldly devalued the contributions they made over the course of a lifetime.

When her father kissed her good-night, he passed on some words of advice. "I know life dealt you an unfair hand, honey, but remember, Bryce is a good man and time really does heal all wounds."

Too tired to expend the energy to argue, she quipped, "If only it would wound all heels."

She patted his hand lovingly and was surprised at its papery texture.

"Just don't go getting your hopes up for something that's not ever going to materialize, Dad."

Gillian headed back the same way she'd come, wondering all the while how she was going to manage being confined in close quarters with the only man she'd ever loved and hated with equal measure.

When she returned to the family room, she was grateful to find a fresh log on the fire and the room empty. All she had to do now was slip into bed without disturbing Bryce.

And letting him slip uninvited into her dreams.

Seven

Bryce saw little need to stoke the fire before turning in. Just thinking about how sexy Gillian looked in those ridiculous pink long johns made him hot all over. Frustrated by his lack of willpower, he figured the smartest thing he could do was to forget about his ex's luscious body, tuck himself into bed and fall sound asleep for the next ten or twelve hours. He doubted that would prove too difficult after a day in which he'd been more successful outrunning an avalanche than his emotions.

It didn't take him long to unpack the few things he'd brought along. Since he preferred sleeping in the nude, he hadn't minded that there wasn't room to pack pajamas. Slipping between the cold sheets of John's king-size bed, he was surprised when sleep eluded him in spite of his exhaustion. He'd hoped to be blissfully unconscious before Gillian returned to rattle his world through walls that were too thin to protect him from his own wicked imagination.

Moonlight filtered through the window, illuminating one of many pictures of Virginia Baron scattered throughout the house. A woman of striking good looks, she exuded the same aura of gentleness that first attracted Bryce to her daughter. Had she lived, Bryce wondered if she could have somehow managed to do for Gillian what he himself could not: coax her out of the same grave in which they'd buried Bonnie. Bryce thought it tragic that John never found anyone to take his beloved wife's place. What a terrible waste that such a vibrant man couldn't bring himself to remarry.

Bryce supposed it was different when the love of one's life preceded a spouse in death—as opposed to having her rip your heart out while she was still very much alive. Vi may not stir his blood the way Gillian did—and still could if his reaction to her in a pair of long johns was any indication—but she loved and appreciated him as he was. She didn't expect him to be in two places at once.

Or to be perfect.

Vi was the kind of woman who put her child's welfare above her own. The kind of woman who felt secure enough about their relationship to let him go on a cockamamy holiday pilgrimage without making a big deal about it. Bryce thought she might even forgive him for the kiss he'd shared with Gillian, considering it an impulsive act of a man just happy to be alive after outrunning an avalanche. Nevertheless, he had no intention of hurting Vi by divulging that particular bit of information.

She deserved better. Staring at the ceiling in the dark, Bryce promised himself that she would get it, too. That ill-advised kiss would be his one and only indiscretion.

The sound of drawers opening and closing next door tested that newly minted vow. Hearing Gillian reacquaint herself with her old room, Bryce couldn't help but wonder what she was wearing. Was she still filling out those long johns with enticing womanly curves? Or had she found some sexy nightie hanging in her closet? Was she sleeping in the nude like him?

Long after she'd turned off the lights next door, Bryce lay awake thinking. When sleep finally settled heavily on his eyelids, it was only to torment his dreams with a demon with amethyst-colored eyes.

* * *

Bryce wasn't the only one who had trouble sleeping that night. Gillian thrashed so wildly beneath her covers that she awoke shortly after falling asleep. Bathed in sweat, she emerged from her night terrors and sat up in bed, disoriented. She was shaking all over.

"So much blood…" she mumbled, reliving the nightmare all over again.

In her dream Virginia Baron had been young, beautiful and very much alive. And very excited about throwing her youngest daughter a baby shower. Surrounded by balloons and decorations, Gillian smiled as she opened present after present. One was a beautiful receiving blanket that her mother had painstakingly made by hand. When Gillian showed it to Bryce so he could get a better look at the unicorn so intricately embroidered on its satin cover, it ripped in two. That was when Gillian knew that something was wrong with her baby. She started screaming…and screaming.…

Gillian covered her mouth with a pillow. The last thing she needed was for Bryce to hear her crying and rush in to see what was the matter. Fighting the urge to seek comfort in his arms, Gillian tried to calm herself down.

"There's nothing to be afraid of. It was just a bad dream," she whispered into the dark.

"You can always have more children. Remember?"

Although Gillian had disavowed motherhood altogether after Bonnie's death, time had a way of healing the spirit and renewing old dreams. Seeing Bryce in that snapshot with Vi and Robbie had awakened in her a longing that was even stronger than her grief. She admired his willingness to take on another man's child as his own and seriously allowed herself to consider adoption for the first time. Feeling somewhat hopeful, she slid back under the covers and fell into a deep sleep untroubled by anything more than the haunting memory of a kiss exchanged in the swirl of falling snowflakes.

Gillian awakened refreshed the next morning to the smell of fresh coffee, bacon and pancakes. She could think of only one better way to start the day, but since the prospects of a long, lovely bout of love-making were nil, she gave herself over to her growling stomach with excitement. It couldn't remember the last time she'd eaten anything for breakfast other than cold cereal or some lousy fast food grabbed on the way to work. Without pausing to do her makeup, Gillian donned a pair of jeans, pulled on a sweater the color of pink carnations, and headed downstairs.

Looking more like his old self after a good night's

sleep, John Baron greeted his daughter with a fork poised halfway between his plate and his lips.

"Good morning, sleepyhead," he said.

Gillian sniffed the air appreciatively. "Morning, Daddy."

She was surprised to see Bryce standing over the stove flipping flapjacks with an expertise that he must have mastered sometime after the divorce. She didn't remember him having any proclivity for cooking while they were married. Taking her seat at the table, she said as much.

"Good morning to you, too," he said, taking umbrage at her observation.

He approached her with a stack of pancakes hot from the griddle and waved them under her nose.

"Anybody hassling the cook can always forgo breakfast altogether," he suggested.

"I'll be quiet," Gillian assured him as she stuck a fork in the top pancake and dropped it onto her plate.

A moment later, she complimented him through a mouthful of melted butter and maple syrup.

"This is good. Delicious in fact."

Sunshine poured through the window filling the kitchen with a sense of holiday cheer. A feeling of déjà vu came over Gillian as she was transported to a point in her marriage when fresh coffee, good food, small talk and fond touches were the way she normally started the day. Imbued with a rare feeling that all was well with the world, she gave herself permission to enjoy the moment without second-guessing her feelings.

Only after everyone at the table enjoyed a second helping did Bryce broach the subject of why the two of them made the trip to the ranch.

"This seems as good a time as any to discuss whatever it is you wanted to talk to us about, John."

John agreed. "I don't suppose it's any secret that Rose and Stella want me to sell the ranch and move into town, presumably in an assisted-living community or old folks' home so they'll get their inheritance."

Gillian laid her fork down and opened her mouth to argue with him, but John didn't give her the chance to mince over his choice of words.

"Which I understand is pretty sizable if rumors about the value of this property hold true. As a realtor, that's something I'd expect you to check into, Gillian."

Nodding, she let him continue without interruption.

"Your sisters and I have already had words about what they consider my 'erratic behavior,' and they didn't like what I had to say on the matter. They're under the impression that I'm some doddering old fool who can be manipulated at will. That they're in such a dither about the two of you sharing durable power of attorney for me tells me that my suspicions about their motives aren't entirely unfounded."

"To be fair, I can understand how they might perceive an outsider like me as a threat," Bryce said. "I already told Gillian I'd be more than happy to take my name off any official documents and let you and your daughters handle your own affairs without any interference from me."

Gillian was taken aback when Bryce interjected on behalf of two people she knew he despised.

"You're no outsider!" John exploded. "Don't you know I think of you as a son?"

He wasn't saying anything that Gillian didn't already know. Still, as much as she once appreciated the closeness between these two men, it was hard not to resent it now that she was divorced. Didn't her father have any faith in *her* ability to handle such matters without Bryce looking over her shoulder? Didn't he realize what an awkward position he was putting her in, pitting sibling against sibling and ex-wife against ex-husband?

Bryce was clearly moved by the disclosure, but since neither man was one to linger over sentimental feelings, John simply cleared his throat before continuing.

"I want you two to take as much time as you need to look through my books and determine the state of my mental and physical health without any outside interference from anyone. And when you're done, I have a little proposition for you."

Gillian braced herself. Sharing a leery look with Bryce, she heard an old line from a movie playing in the back of her mind.

I'm gonna make you an offer you can't refuse....

Eight

It came as no surprise to Gillian that her father was less than forthcoming about his little "proposition." An expert horse trader, the man had mastered the art of suspense long ago. John Baron wouldn't be rushed. He flatly declined to explain himself any further other than to say he'd be glad to continue the conversation when she and Bryce had all the information they needed. Then he left them alone to proceed as they saw fit.

Although naturally better with words than with numbers, Gillian was savvy enough to read a balance sheet and decipher the story inherent in the figures.

From what Stella inferred about their father's recent wild spending habits, she half expected to find the ranch hovering on the edge of bankruptcy. A thorough examination of the books reassured her that the situation wasn't nearly as dire as that.

Although her father had always been generous, in the past year her father had donated large sums to just about every charity imaginable and set up a healthy pension fund for Dustin and Bette. In addition he'd set up a renewable scholarship in his wife's name for high school graduates interested in pursuing a degree in agriculture. He'd also discovered eBay and was spending a small fortune on antique coins and collectibles. In spite of the healthy bite this all took out of his monthly living expenses, John's own needs appeared to be quite simple. Truthfully Gillian wished he would spend more of his hard-earned money on himself instead of everybody else.

After hours of scouring the books, Bryce leaned back in a red-tooled leather chair and announced, "Your sisters might not approve of what your father is doing with his expendable income, but it looks like everything is accounted for. Even taking into consideration any questionable expenses, the ranch appears to be doing well. I see no reason why it can't sustain itself for many years to come."

Gillian nodded in agreement.

"We should probably look into some of those charitable foundations," she suggested, "just to make sure they're legitimate. Maybe we can persuade him to focus his spending on those causes that have the greatest need and use their contributions most wisely."

When Bryce stood up and stretched, his tight-fitting jeans and dark turtleneck did little to hide his muscles from her feminine appraisal.

"Listen, Gill," he said, looking her straight in the eyes. "I need you to be honest with me. Are you or are you not on board with Rose and Stella's plan to sell the ranch and live off the profits?"

Although insulted by the question, Gillian did her best to respond in a level tone, knowing she hadn't given Bryce much reason to think she didn't agree with her sisters. "I just want what's best for my father."

Bryce looked at her skeptically. "It wouldn't take much to convince your father to sell out to a developer, and you'd never have to work again. You could be living the high life instead of slogging through day after dreary day of showing housing and putting up with unreasonable clients."

Gillian's eyes snapped with indignation as she leaped to her feet.

"Look, you don't have to tell me that selling this

ranch is the last thing he wants to do, but there's more to consider than just the books. I have to think about his health, too. It's all well and fine for you to stand here and accuse me of being an unfit daughter. None of this will matter to you once you're back home. I'm the one who'll be worried sick when I'm hundreds of miles away wondering whether he's fallen and broken a hip."

Unmoved by the emotional fervor her voice had taken, Bryce broke into her tirade with cold, hard logic.

"What about modern technological wonders like alert monitors?" he asked.

"They're wonderful if you live in a city," Gillian pointed out. "Are you forgetting how long it would take for help to get here even in ideal circumstances?"

"Home health care is always an option."

Gillian rolled her eyes. "Do you want to be the one who suggests that?"

A personal nurse wouldn't last more than a week with a man as fiercely independent and contrary as her father.

"What if, to save his pride, we were to call it 'house-keeping services'?" Bryce proposed. "Complete with a cook to make sure he eats right, too?"

It wasn't a bad idea. And Gillian would have given it more thought had not another modern technological wonder interrupted the discussion as Bryce reached for his cell phone. She noted how his facial expression immediately softened when he discovered Vi was the caller.

"It's good to hear your voice."

Gillian tried to make the hard lump forming in the pit of her stomach go away by telling herself that by all rights, she was indebted to this woman for letting Bryce come here at all. If she could only stop hating her for a minute, Gillian supposed she might actually like Vi under other circumstances.

"I'm fine," Bryce said. "Everything's fine, but until we get John's affairs settled and it's safe to travel, I'm just not sure how much longer I'm going to be stuck here."

Stuck here with her, he meant.

The saliva in Gillian's mouth congealed at his choice of words. Swallowing became impossible when he asked about Robbie.

The ugly truth was that Gillian felt far more threatened by that darling little boy than his mother. Seeing how Gillian had been the one to file for divorce, she knew how utterly unfair it would be to begrudge Bryce another woman's companionship. However, Robbie was an entirely different matter. The idea of him adopting a child to replace Bonnie left a steel blade protruding out of her back.

"Tell him I'll do my very best to get him to that

Nuggets game." There was only a short pause before he added, "I miss you, too."

Gillian made a beeline for the door, she didn't want to hear him tell another woman that he loved her. Besides it was hard not to resent how eager he was to return to Vi. She remembered how hard it used to be getting Bryce to take any time off from work to make time for Bonnie and her.

Having averaged over sixty hours a week at work herself over the past year, she had a better understanding now of the work ethic that had put such a strain on their marriage. It struck her as odd that Bryce hadn't so much as mentioned his business since embarking on this journey, let alone obsessing about it the way he used to. Although she couldn't quite put her finger on it, there were an awful lot of ways that he seemed different from the man she remembered. It wasn't just that he'd grown so hard toward her, either. He seemed more sure of himself, more comfortable in his own skin. Maybe it was because he'd finally made it to the top of his field that he seemed more relaxed and at peace with himself.

Safely away from his conversation with Vi, Gillian took the opportunity to call her sisters and leave messages for them letting them know that she'd arrived safely. She suspected that neither one of them would be happy to hear that she was snowed in for an indefinite length of time with their ex-brother-in-law, so she deliberately didn't mention it. Hoping to delay a confrontation with them until she had all the facts about their dad together, she made another call to the family doctor inquiring about her father's general health.

"He'll probably outlive us both," Dr. Schuler told her. "That's not to say that hiring someone to look after him isn't a good idea. And I'll run some tests for Alzheimer's if you still want me to."

Gillian thanked him before hanging up. She wondered how her sisters would feel about his prognosis or if they would insist on a second opinion.

The remainder of the day passed without a harsh word spoken between Bryce and her. Having accounted for the books, they set up conference calls with lawyers, bankers and home care agencies to try to come up with some way for John to remain at the ranch and allow those who loved him to rest easy.

When dinnertime finally rolled around, Gillian's brain was mush. Earlier Bryce had taken three big T-bones out of the freezer. While they were marinating, he scooped a path through the snow to the propane grill on the back deck. Gillian contributed to the meal by preparing a fresh salad and throwing some potatoes into the microwave. When her father finally emerged from his bedroom, he was greeted by the smell of his favorite dinner.

"It's been a long time since I've eaten so well," he said, savoring each and every bite over the clicking of his dentures.

Gillian was happy to see he had an appetite. He ate everything she put in front of him, making her wonder if he'd been eating little but what could conveniently be dumped out of a can and warmed up in a saucepan. She also noticed that his hands shook when he held out his plate for more. When he finally pushed himself away from the table, it was to announce that he was glad the books met with their approval.

"I really do want to discuss some business matters with you, but I'm feeling a little too tired and too full right now so, if you don't mind, I'll turn in early tonight and we can talk about it tomorrow."

"Sure, Dad." Gillian's head hurt from crunching numbers all day and trying to come up with a creative solution that would satisfy her sisters while still leaving her father's pride intact.

She walked him back to his room where Padre was waiting. The poor old thing was barely able to lift his head off his paws in greeting.

After safely helping her father into his recliner, Gillian took a hard look at the man who had always been her rock. Etched into John Baron's weathered face was a lifetime of hardship and love. Marred by age spots, the wrinkled hands that patted the top of

Padre's head were the same ones that had held her as an infant and provided sympathy at his granddaughter's funeral. She was suddenly flooded with love for the remarkable man who had built an empire on little more than sheer determination and hard work.

"Did I ever tell you what an amazing job you've done maintaining the ranch all these years and raising three kids all on your own after Mom died?"

Her father looked so perplexed by the compliment that Gillian regretted not having told him more often. She always assumed he knew how she felt.

"Don't you think it's time you allowed somebody else to take on the burdens of running this place?" she asked gently. "Have you given any thought at all to asking for a little help?"

"Once in a while," he admitted through a tired smile. "It's been a good life. I've been lucky to thoroughly enjoy what I do. If there's anything I regret, it's only that I don't have any grandchildren to pass my legacy on to."

Gillian knew that he didn't mean to be cruel, but those words cut like barbed wire. Didn't he know that there was nothing *she* would have liked more than to give him a grandchild? Bowing her head, she turned away to hide her pained expression.

"Night, night," she said, employing the same phrase he'd used to tuck her in at night until she'd become too old for such nonsense. The same sweet words she'd whispered to Bonnie every night for the short, precious time she'd been on the planet.

Fighting off a pervasive sense of melancholy, Gillian ambled back to the main part of the house where Bryce was engaged in a battle with a string of Christmas lights that appeared to be tangled beyond help. She'd almost forgotten that Christmas would be here in two days whether she was ready for it or not. It didn't appear as though they were going to get out of here tomorrow as originally planned. The last place she ever expected to be spending the holidays was in her girlhood home with her ex-husband, but all of a sudden that didn't sound nearly as awful as spending it all alone. Doubting there would ever be a better time to let go of any lingering animosity between them, she offered her services to the cause.

"What can I do to help?"

"You could pour me a stiff drink before I strangle myself with these lights," Bryce told her.

Gillian obliged by unearthing a bottle of fine Riesling from a full wine rack in the pantry. She poured a generous portion into two goblets and proposed a toast.

"To Christmas."

They clinked glasses and shared the taste of a

vintage year. Soon Gillian was digging a tree stand out of one of the boxes Bryce brought down from the attic earlier. Positioning it in the traditional place of honor in front of the big picture window, she helped him settle the tree inside and line it up. For her efforts she suffered the indignity of pine needles stuck in her hair. Bryce helped comb them out with his fingers.

When she felt his touch, Gillian had to remind herself to breathe. Embarrassed to be so utterly flummoxed by such a simple courtesy, she quickly gave her attention to a cluster of lights heaped in the middle of the floor. With an efficiency that made his business so successful, Bryce started unraveling one end and directed her to start the other. Some of the knots were more intricate than others, but it didn't take long for their patience to pay off. With all the arguing they'd being doing, Gillian had forgotten how well they worked together.

If only it were as simple to untangle our lives as a string of lights, she thought with a sigh.

After wrapping the tree with twinkling bulbs, they proceeded to unpack several dusty boxes of ornaments. Each evoked a special memory: some were given to Gillian as gifts, some she'd made as a child for her parents and some commemorated special events in her life. Those made of handblown glass were bona fide antiques and would fetch an impressive price at an antique shop. Those more sentimental in nature were priceless.

"Oh, no!" Gillian exclaimed, holding up a crystal snowflake that had broken in the box. A present from her mother shortly before her death, it was very dear to her.

"How could someone be so careless?" she wondered aloud.

Bryce's eyes clouded over as he seemed to consider the question on many levels. Coming to stand beside her, he explained, "Sometimes we simply forget to take care of the things most precious to us."

Gillian's defenses crumbled beneath that subtle apology. There were things she had failed to take proper care of, as well—like her husband's need to provide for his family and the baby she'd put down for a nap, never imagining the unthinkable could happen.

The damaged ornament slipped from her hand and shattered as it hit the floor.

"And sometimes," Bryce said, tipping her chin up so she was forced to look at him, "things happen that are out of our control, leaving us no choice but to accept them and move on."

The multicolored lights on the Christmas tree blurred in the reflection of Gillian's unshed tears.

"What if I can't?" she asked in a choked whisper.

Gathering her in his arms, he cradled her against

him as the emotion finally burst through the dam that had held everything back for so long.

"Go ahead and get it all out, sweetheart," Bryce urged softly.

"What's wrong with me?" she asked in between sobs. "Why can't I let go of the pain like you?"

"Maybe you're just still mad at God."

"Why shouldn't I be?" she demanded to know. "What kind of monster would take an innocent baby from her mother?"

"And her father..."

Gillian nodded. Having felt her baby's heart beat beneath her own for nine months, she tended to forget that tragedy touched both of them.

Bryce paused before attempting to answer the impossible question she'd put to him.

"I don't think God's a monster. He also gave us one another. I'm sorry that wasn't enough to get us through that terrible loss."

Gillian drew back angrily. "I don't need to hear any religious platitudes from the same man who placed the needs of his business over those of his wife and daughter."

"I did the best I could at the time," Bryce said, holding her against his heart. "You have to believe that."

Deep down, Gillian knew Bryce hurt as much as

she did and regretted her outburst. "I know," she conceded in a broken whisper. "We both did, but it wasn't good enough to save our baby."

Gillian fully expected Bryce to blame her as much as she blamed herself. However she tried spinning the events of the past, she was the one responsible for Bonnie's death. All the times she'd laid blame at Bryce's feet for not being there when she most needed him, she had really been railing at herself.

She never should have taken a nap while the baby was sleeping.

She shouldn't have panicked and wasted precious time before dialing 911.

She should have taken a course in infant CPR before ever taking Bonnie home from the hospital.

She should have found some way to keep her baby alive until help arrived.

Bryce's angry voice sliced through her guilt. "Stop looking for blame, Gill. It wasn't anybody's fault. Nobody holds you accountable—least of all me."

As he wiped the tears from her face, a sad smile played with the corners of Gillian's lips.

"How did I ever let you go?" she wanted to know.

"I didn't go willingly," he reminded her, then sighed and added philosophically, "but what's done is done. Beyond finally finding closure, there isn't much point in belaboring what's happened in the past."

When he bent down to deposit a platonic kiss on the tip of her nose, Gillian was seized by a fierceness of emotion. She lifted her head so that his lips met hers and poured her heart into a kiss that didn't just stop the world from spinning on its axis. It completely reversed its rotation.

He tasted of fine wine and pure redemption. Gillian dragged her fingers through the soft hair at his nape. She didn't know exactly what she was starting, and she didn't care. Incapable of rational thought, she had no grand scheme attached to her actions. The only thing she knew for sure was that she didn't want to face another night alone.

Nine

Gillian was no fool. She didn't expect whatever was going to happen next to alter anything between them permanently. She wasn't out to steal her man back from Vi, nor did she intend to demand any more from Bryce than he could offer. She just desperately needed him for the night.

One harmless body-and-soul-melting night.

Filling her lungs with his all too-familiar masculine scent, she felt a slow, steady tug in her belly. It reminded her how much she missed the feel of a man's skin hot against hers. Being with Bryce resurrected in Gillian the sensual being she'd thought long dead. She wanted to run her hands through the variegated strands of gold that were interspersed in his dark hair and lose herself in a bout of mindless sex.

Slipping trembling fingers beneath the weave of his shirt, she was relieved to find that her touch still could make him shiver. She was thrilled to feel his heart beating out a wild cadence against the palm of her hand.

Gillian doubted that Bryce had remained celibate since their divorce.

As she had. Although she'd dated since their divorce, Gillian hadn't met anyone for whom she'd been able to feel the same intense emotions Bryce evoked in her. Physically she wanted to be with a man, if anything to help her put Bryce behind her, but she hadn't been able to get her heart to listen to her head.

Shoving aside that thought, she told herself not to overthink her actions for once in her life. After all, this wasn't rocket science. She wanted this man. And needed him like never before.

She dismissed that "be careful playing with fire" look glittering in Bryce's eyes with a "Don't worry. I'm a big girl" look of her own. Anticipation thrummed through her entire being as she tilted her face toward his and claimed his lips an instant later with a possessiveness that belied her promise to give him up willingly later.

Gillian took her time exploring his sensual mouth, which insisted the present was the only thing worth living for. Giving herself completely over to that belief, she pressed herself against the long, hard length of his body and welcomed the responding pressure of his erection. Her pulse vibrated in her ears. Her head began to swirl. And sparks exploded behind her eyes.

It was impossible to get enough of each other.

They clung to each other beneath the twinkling Christmas lights and the watchful eyes of the angel topping the tree. Dropping her head into the safe hollow of Bryce's shoulder, Gillian felt truly at home for the first time in years.

Unfortunately that sense of security lasted only a moment before he took her firmly by both shoulders, pushed her away and put an end to any fleeting fantasy about picking up where they left off.

"I didn't cheat on you when we were married, and I'm not going to cheat on Vi when we're about to become husband and wife," he said, wiping the kiss from his lips with the back of his hand.

Blood roared in Gillian's ears and the heat of shame settled on her cheeks. She imagined Bryce was taking a good measure of enjoyment from seeing her so vulnerable and needy.

So hurt.

So utterly pathetic in light of his high-minded refusal to her no-strings-attached offer of sex.

Thoroughly humiliated, Gillian scrambled to find any words that might help put her degradation behind her. Covering her mouth with her hand, she took a step backward. Looking him in the eye was one of the hardest things she'd ever had to do.

"I'm sorry," she said. "About everything. For dragging you back into my family's problems, for embarrassing both of us just now, for being such a bad mother. But most of all for hurting you. I hope you can believe that."

Feeling his resolve chipping away, Bryce told himself that he couldn't afford to be entranced by those hypnotic eyes again, even if they were misting over with tears. Finding it impossible not to be moved by her beauty, he was amazed he'd ever found the strength to push her away at all. She was still as lovely as the day he'd taken her to his bed as an innocent bride. Only now her face was marked by a woman's rite of passage: the splendor of finding love, the transformation of a daughter into a wife and the unspeakable agony of losing an infant. It was a face no man could ever forget.

"You were a wonderful mother. This has nothing to do with that," he said gruffly, unable to stand the thought of her going through life thinking she wasn't.

Gillian gave her head a self-deprecating shake as she continued to back away.

"I certainly didn't feel like it at the time. I was so tired and cranky and out of sorts most days trying to juggle your demanding schedule with Bonnie's needs. Needs that always seemed to take priority over yours. And my own for that matter. Looking back, I'm sure I was impossible to live with. No wonder you don't want anything to do with me."

"A little hormonal maybe," he grudgingly agreed. "But not impossible."

At the time Bryce had deeply resented Gillian's lack of interest in his career, as well as her being too exhausted most nights to do little more in bed than promptly fall asleep. Looking back it was far easier to put into perspective what she must have been going through as a young mother.

"I'm sorry I wasn't more sensitive to *your* needs," Bryce said, remembering days when he was actually relieved to go to the office and leave her with the colicky baby. "Even though we were both over-whelmed and doing the best we could at the time, you'll never know how bad I felt about being out of town when…"

He was unable to finish the sentence. Images of his baby girl in her crib and his wife frantically doing everything in her power to breathe the soul back into her lifeless body left him feeling powerless. Guilt-ridden.

"I should have been there."

In light of his rejection to her advances, he was astonished when she offered him the last thing he ever expected from her. Absolution.

"It wouldn't have made any difference. It was wrong of me to blame you—it was just so much easier than blaming myself. That day, when I closed my eyes for such a short time after putting Bonnie down for a nap, it never occurred to me that that would be the last time...."

The crack in her voice matched the one that broke Bryce's heart in two. He put a finger to her lips to stop her from continuing.

"Enough," he said. "We can't go on beating ourselves up over this. Probably the only thing we should have done differently was have this conversation sooner."

They'd both been so wrapped up in their grief at the time that neither could break through the other's barriers. It wasn't long before they'd stopped talking about everything altogether.

"I know you're afraid to have more children, but there's no reason that you shouldn't," he said. "There's no evidence that SIDS is genetic. The doctors told you that you could have as many healthy, happy, beautiful children as you want to. And you should."

Gillian shook her head sadly. "I haven't had the same luck moving on with my life as you have."

"You will," Bryce told her with the same optimism that marked his business acumen.

She wished she could believe him. As good as it felt to clear the air between them and as much as she appreciated his kind words, she just couldn't see herself ever getting married again. The few dates she'd gone on after the divorce were mostly miserable setups by well-meaning friends attempting to play matchmaker. The strained conversations generated by such dates only served to convince Gillian that she wasn't ready to move on yet.

It was strange to think that she and Bryce might still be together had they only been able to talk like this before for surely it had been the lack of communication between them as much as Bonnie's death that had led to the demise of their marriage. In retrospect Gillian was sorry she hadn't taken more interest in his business when he'd been working so hard to make it a success. She wished she'd made more time for the two of them as a couple instead of focusing all her energies on the baby and being more a mother than a wife.

As much as she hated to put an end to this meaningful albeit painful exchange, Bryce had made himself perfectly clear about "saving" himself for Vi, leaving Gillian no other choice but to respect him for that. The last thing she wanted to do was ruin their temporary truce by accidentally saying the wrong thing.

Like how sorry she was for ever letting him go.

"I suppose we should call it a day," she said, moving toward the stairs.

"I'll come with you," Bryce called after her.

Still stinging from his earlier rebuke, Gillian refrained from mentioning how disappointed she was that they were sleeping in separate beds. With every step they took up those stairs, the poison of old bitterness drained from her body. It occurred to her that while she had no control over the past, how she lived the present was truly up to her. She could live each day as bitterly as Stella who had never gotten over the humiliation of her ex-husband's indiscretions. Or as lonely as Rose who was still pining for some mythical knight to come charging into her life astride a white horse. Or as a woman able to forgive herself and others for their mistakes.

She and Bryce paused at the landing to survey the scene below. A fire crackled in a hearth decorated with stockings, ornaments glittered amid shimmering Christmas lights and the smell of pine hung heavy in the air. A peaceful feeling settled over Gillian.

Standing on tiptoe, she ventured to place a chaste peck on Bryce's cheek. Marked by the stubble of a day's growth, it felt rough against her lips.

"I hope Vi knows how incredibly lucky she is," she said before turning and closing her bedroom door firmly behind her.

Ten

There was no pounding at the front door the next morning to alert anyone that the house was under assault. No sirens or alarms went off. The intruders simply opened the front door and walked in as if they owned the place.

"Surprise!" they hollered.

It wasn't long before the sound of tramping feet signaled that the invasion had come upstairs. The force with which the bedroom doors were flung open would lead one to think the Secret Service had arrived with a warrant for a deadly criminal. Gillian came to with a jerk. Standing in the doorway of her bedroom was her oldest sister Stella looking as if she had just swallowed a case of TNT.

"What are you doing here?" Gillian asked as she clamored out of bed and grabbed a robe.

The shriek down the hallway prevented Stella from answering. The two of them rushed to where Gillian's other sister Rose was cemented in the threshold of Bryce's bedroom, an expression of horror on her face. The exact same question that Gillian had just posed to Stella leaped out of her mouth.

"What are you doing in Dad's room?" she demanded of the naked man who was occupying her father's bed.

Suddenly grateful that her plan for seducing Bryce last night hadn't actually materialized, Gillian imagined their reaction to discovering her in bed with Bryce would probably register on the Richter scale.

Roused from a state of deep sleep, the man of the hour sat up, looking completely disoriented. He rubbed the exhaustion from his eyes as if to rid himself of a recurring nightmare. He then folded his hands behind his head, allowing the sheet to drop away from his torso and puddle around his waist.

"To what do I owe the honor of this intrusion?" he asked.

A blush the same shade as her name crept up Rose's neck and settled upon her plump cheeks. She looked everywhere but at Bryce's deliciously bare chest. Gillian wasn't so shy. Even on the brink of a family feud, it was impossible not to appreciate all of that masculine glory rumbling to life.

"What are you doing sleeping in here?" Stella asked.

Gillian thought Bryce made a better big, bad bear than poor Goldilocks as her sister continued pressing for answers.

"What have you done with him?"

More amused than insulted by the question, he had the audacity to chuckle. "Didn't you check the freezer before rushing up here?"

Gillian threw herself between him and her sisters when she saw the look of horror on their faces.

"He's moved into the downstairs bedroom off the den," she explained.

"I can't believe you had the gall to move poor Daddy out of his bedroom just so you could—"

Gillian hastened to interrupt before matters got any more out of hand.

"He made the decision all on his own long before we ever arrived. He says he can't handle the stairs anymore."

Although irritated at having to explain herself, she was at the same time relieved to discover she wasn't the only one in the family who hadn't been informed of her father's change in living quarters.

That simple revelation made her somehow feel less negligent as a daughter. For all her sisters' ranting about how worried they were about his welfare, they were just as clueless as she was about the daily goings-on of their father's life. Which made her question on what they were basing their assessments of his health.

"Thank God we got here before…"

Gillian wasn't a child, and Stella's dangling implication didn't sit well with her.

"Before what?"

"Before I could coerce you back into my bed," Bryce filled in, dropping all pretense of nicety. "It's hard to believe you two showed up today out of any real desire to spend Christmas Day as a family. I have a sneaking suspicion that what you're really concerned about is your own pocketbook, and that's something you'll have to take up with John, not me. So if you *ladies* would excuse me, I'd like to get dressed before continuing this conversation downstairs."

When the sisters refused to budge, he threw a bare leg out from under the covers as a prelude of what was to come, causing Rose to squeak and back out of the room as fast as she could. Stella was harder to persuade. Gathering her indignation about her like a robe, she informed Gillian, "If you have any sense of decency at all, you'll follow us!"

Although she knew Stella was right, Gillian was sorely tempted to see what Bryce was hiding under the covers. With a sigh, she smiled at him before turning and giving him his privacy.

It was hard, if not downright impossible, for Bryce not to savor the irony of the situation. He wouldn't trade the memory of the horrified expressions on the faces of his ex-sisters-in-law for anything. It was priceless. He harbored no illusion about ever convincing either Rose or Stella that he wasn't trying to orchestrate some licentious scene involving their little sister all the while trying to get his hooks into their daddy's money. He had as much hope of doing that as he had convincing Gillian that her sisters simply wanted to have their father committed so they could have free access to his fortune.

Bryce was happy that his obligation lay with John Baron instead of anyone else in the family. Considering how his own father had been so emotionally and physically distant so much of his life, Bryce supposed it was only natural that he would come to think of Gillian's dad as more than just a mentor and friend. His ex-father-in-law had been the only member of the Baron clan to support him during the terrible days when his marriage and his life were falling apart. If there was a hell on earth, surely it existed for those parents who have lost a child. Bryce would be forever in John Baron's debt for all he'd done to make the pain of that unspeakable grief a little more bearable.

He couldn't stand the thought of such a good man being mistreated by his own flesh and blood.

Recalling how Rose and Stella had taken every opportunity to imply his heavy work schedule into some kind of deliberate abandonment of Gillian and Bonnie, Bryce took his own sweet time showering and getting dressed before making his way downstairs. Angry voices—the same ones that had plagued him for years—ascended to greet him like steam rising from the depths of a devil's lair. Stepping into the kitchen, he interrupted a heated discussion with a simple question.

"How did the two of you get here? I didn't think the snow coach was running."

Not moved to civility by his attempt to be friendly, Stella snapped, "Same way you did, of course. Prehistorically."

Bryce didn't even try to suppress a grin as he glanced out the window to where two more gleaming snowmobiles were parked in the driveway. Everyone knew how much Stella and Rose despised anything to do with "roughing it." In fact, they'd both opted to attend private boarding schools as soon as they were through junior high whereas Gillian chose to finish high school in Jackson Hole proper after her mother was diagnosed with cancer. Virginia Baron passed away before her youngest daughter finished her freshman year of high school. While her sisters traveled after returning home for the funeral, Gillian remained home, helping her father through the anguish of losing his wife and assisting him with the daily operations of running the ranch. And had truly loved every minute of it. That Bryce's two prima donna ex-sisters-in-law would strap themselves on a snowmobile under such arduous conditions was proof enough of just how desperate they must be.

"Part of the trail was cleared late yesterday. It's barely passable now and the snow coaches won't be running until after Christmas," Rose explained. "The ride in was terrible. It's a wonder we made it at all."

"Which just goes to show how utterly ridiculous it is for Daddy to remain here, cut off from all civilization," Stella added with an indignant sniff.

She winced when Bryce joined them at the kitchen table after pouring himself a cup of coffee.

"Are you sure you didn't arrange for Daddy to move into the farthest corner of this house just so you could have some special time to sink your claws back into your Gillian and try to turn her against us—"

"Stop it!"

The same booming voice that had once ruled over a houseful of querulous teenage girls ended the conversation with an unquestioned air of authority. Shaking his head in disgust, John Baron stared at his contentious brood.

"Merry Christmas, Daddy!"

Stella and Rose jumped out of their chairs and rushed to envelop him in a hug. He reveled in their enthusiastic embrace before asking, "What are you two doing here? You can't be bothered to visit when the weather's good?"

If Bryce had any doubts about the old man's competence, they quickly evaporated as John proceeded to prove that he was perfectly capable of taking care of himself. Leaning back in his chair, he watched to see how Stella and Rose were going to attempt to convince the crafty, old codger that he wasn't in complete control of his faculties.

Rose responded with a hurt expression.

"We thought it would be a nice surprise to drop in on you for the holidays," Stella explained.

Harrumphing, John gave her a steely look.

"If I had wanted you two to join us here, I would have asked you. Frankly what I want to discuss with your sister and Bryce is none of your business."

"You can't possibly mean that!"

Her father's expression softened at the sight of Rose's tears.

"That's not to say that I'm not happy to have you girls all together for the holidays. I can't remember the last time we celebrated Christmas Day as a family. Actually, this probably will work out for the best after all. It's just that I wanted to run my ideas past Bryce and Gillian before involving the rest of you in my decision. And mind you, it is *my* decision."

The room grew jarringly quiet as he cleared his throat and turned to address his oldest daughters.

"Since you two are convinced that I'm incapable of remaining here on my own, and neither one of you have ever bothered to hide the fact that you want nothing to do with running this ranch, it is my intention to give it to Gillian and Bryce jointly."

Eleven

"And a Merry Christmas to you, too, Daddy!" Stella exclaimed angrily in reaction to that little bombshell.

Rose dragged the back of one arm across her puffy face and whimpered, "You can't possibly mean that."

Before Gillian could turn away in embarrassment, Stella pointed a bony finger in her face.

"You always were Daddy's little darling. I'll bet you've been planning this for years. Probably ever since you tied up with…with…that gold digger!"

She said it as if this were the worst name she could think of. Watching Stella lash out indiscriminately reminded Gillian of the time she'd accidentally disturbed a nest of rattlesnakes. She'd been shocked and scared at the time and was very careful when she retreated in case one of the snakes lashed out and bit her.

Unable to believe what she was hearing, she had to ask, "Do I need to remind you that Bryce and I are divorced? And you're the one who insisted I convince him to come here with me in the first place? Have you forgotten how strongly I objected to *that* suggestion?"

"That's right," Rose chimed in. "I warned you that it was a mistake to involve him, Stell."

"Like I had any choice in the matter," she retorted. "The codicil that Dad attached to the will makes it virtually impossible to do anything without Bryce's consent."

Reminded of their father's shocking decision in the matter, Rose decided to direct her fury at the only person in the room who appeared to be enjoying her histrionics.

"You're no longer a part of this family," she yelled at Bryce. "Truth be told, you never were."

Though a flicker of pain darkened Bryce's blue eyes, it was her father's reaction that most worried Gillian. His face was growing redder by the second, and a purple vein in his forehead throbbed threateningly. If her sisters truly were as concerned about his health as they claimed, they would deal with this situation calmly and not be pushing him to have a heart attack.

"I've had just about enough of this nonsense!" he roared. "Do I have to remind all of you that you're still in *my* house? I'm not dead yet! And I'm not about to let anybody put me in my grave until I'm good and ready to go there!"

Far from extinguishing the growing blaze of discord, his words seemed to merely throw gas on it.

"You're not being fair!" Stella yelled.

"If you think we won't fight you on this, you'd better think again," Rose added.

Gillian was glad when Bryce posed a question that put the "conversation" back on a more rational track.

"What stipulations are attached to the offer, John?"

The family stopped fighting long enough to hear the answer. Ignoring his daughters' angry expressions, John Baron took a deep breath before looking Bryce squarely in the eye.

"You and Gillian are to run the place together and let me live the rest of my days right here—on this ranch, in this house—for however long that might be."

A stunned silence fell over the room. Gillian cleared her throat uncomfortably.

"You do realize that Bryce and I are divorced and that we don't have any plans of getting back together, don't you?"

Obviously insulted by the implication that he was losing control of his faculties, her father said, "Whoever said anything about you two getting back together? All I said was that I'd like you to run the place. Living arrangements would be up to you—that's nobody else's business. Not mine. And damned sure not your sisters'."

Stella's eyes narrowed with contempt. "Is this about the need to bail out poor Bryce again? Has his business gone under? I warned you not to lend him any money the first time, Daddy, but since you wouldn't listen to me then, I don't expect you will now. I wish you'd just consider the past a valuable learning opportunity and accept that Bryce is never going to make anything of himself—with or without the backing of the Baron money."

Gillian hated that Stella couldn't let Bryce forget that he hadn't been born into the same kind of privileged circumstances they had. Both of her sisters acted as if working for a living was somehow beneath them and had always assumed that Bryce had only married her for their dad's money, which was insulting to both of them.

And as far from the truth as it could be. If anything, Bryce's insistence on building the business on his own had been a sticking point in their marriage. Over his protests, Gillian took the initiative herself and approached her father for the seed money to launch her husband's fledgling company. Bryce had been downright angry when she'd presented him with a signed blank check to finance his entrepreneurial dreams. It had taken all of her womanly finesse to coax him into accepting it as a loan.

John Baron raised a trembling hand and called for quiet. "I'll have you all know that Bryce paid back every penny of that a long time ago. That's a hell of a lot more than I can say about any money I've given anybody else in this room!"

The protests to that observation practically rattled the exposed beams overhead.

"How can you possibly turn your back on us in favor of *him?*" Stella demanded.

Having spent the better part of her marriage defending her sisters to Bryce—they were her sisters after all—Gillian was now embarrassed for them. The fact that they had stepped in to act as a mother for her early after Virginia had been diagnosed with cancer did not absolve them of such behavior. Their vitriolic reaction had her reexamining Bryce's claim that they'd deliberately worked to undermine their marriage. Although she knew that her and Bryce's problems as a couple were of their own making, looking back, she couldn't help but wonder if Rose and Stella may not have intentionally exacerbated them.

Perhaps that was part of the reason she hadn't kept in closer contact with them since the divorce. The thought of three single sisters, who were all mad at the world, hanging out together wasn't exactly Gillian's idea of a fresh start.

As Rose's and Stella's wailing increased in volume, their father took on a more conciliatory tone.

"That's not to say that I'd ever leave any of my girls out in the cold," he assured them. "Considering the financial strain it'll put on the ranch's operating expenses, a million dollars split evenly between Rose and Stella should take care of any objections that either of you might have to my proposal. Did I mention that Gill and Bryce can't sell the place until after I'm dead and gone—which I'm hoping won't be anytime soon? They can divide the ranch however they see fit when that happens, though."

The substantial sum named was enough to put a stop to his daughters' tears momentarily. Rose repeated the sum incredulously.

"A million dollars?"

Stella recovered more quickly. "Moon Cussers is worth ten times more than that!" she protested.

"Only on paper, honey," her father said, wisely shaking his head.

Having spent the last twenty-four hours poring over the ranch's books, Gillian considered that a fair assessment. Her background as a Realtor gave her a good grasp of the staggering figure mentioned.

"Making a ranch this size profitable isn't easy given changing times," she interjected. "It's only worth that extravagant amount you've got in your head if it's sold to a big-time developer. And we all know how Dad feels about that."

"Maybe we could find an environmentally-minded developer?" Rose timidly suggested.

Bryce laughed, but John's eyes took on a steely glint.

"That's my offer," he said in a tone that brooked no compromise. "Take it or leave it."

Gillian felt as if she were being pulled in two by opposing forces. She felt honor-bound to think of her father's best interests above everything else. Having never considered returning to the ranch on a permanent basis, she was surprised how strongly the idea pulled at her. Deep down a part of her did long to return to her home. She also wanted to ensure her father was well taken care of and knew that being here would make that task much easier.

Outside the wind was shaking snow off tree limbs, scattering it like diamonds. Inside, hope landed lightly on Gillian's shoulder. The thought of trying to patch things up with Bryce was tempting. Just being with him these past few days made it hard not to remember why she'd fallen in love with him in the first place.

Was it possible they could start all over again? Maybe even try to start another family?

Bryce had made a point of telling her that she'd been a wonderful mother and reminding her that there was no reason she shouldn't try to have another baby. They— What was she thinking? He'd proposed to another woman and was getting married.

Gillian stammered over the hammering of her heart, "This is too big a decision to make on the spur of the moment. Bryce and I both have our own careers and our own lives to get back to." *No matter how empty and lonely they might be....*

She watched Bryce swallow hard before taking up the cause.

"I can't tell you how much it means that you would entrust me with the ranch that you've spent your entire life building, John. That's not a decision to be made lightly."

Obviously as moved as Gillian was, he seemed to choose his next words carefully.

"But...the truth of the matter is that I'm no cowboy. I'd be completely out of my element trying to follow in your footsteps. As Gillian said, times are changing, and as much as I hate to admit it, the days of working ranches around here are numbered.

Taking that much cash out of your capital to appease your children could very well doom you to bankruptcy. If anything, instead of taking money out of the ranch, I'd recommend you pump more into it and take it in an entirely different direction."

Stella came unglued at that.

"So you not only want our inheritance but our million dollars, too!"

Gillian winced. "Apparently a million dollars is a pittance—until it threatens to disappear altogether," she said, shaking her head in disgust.

Rose appealed to her father on a purely emotional level.

"Can't you see what he's trying to do? He'll tear the entire family apart in no time at all for his own personal gain and ruin everything you've worked so hard for in the process."

"I don't need anybody's money," Bryce said contemptuously. "I'm in the process of selling that little business that you like to speak of so disparagingly. In a couple of months I'll be able to buy this ranch and ten more like it if I want to—I don't have any reason to steal your inheritance. But I'd sure like to repay your father for the faith he put in me when I needed it the most by giving him all the money he needs to run the ranch and put a halt to your cold, calculating proceedings to declare him incompetent."

Gillian thought she could almost hear her father's heart break when he heard Bryce's words. She caught him by the arm as he stumbled reaching for a chair.

"You'd really do that to me?" he asked his daughters, his voice barely audible.

"Of course not!" Rose said less than convincingly.

"H-how could you even think that?" Stella added.

Bryce hastened to assure his old friend. "As long as I have dual power of attorney, I won't allow that to happen. You have my word. And if anyone's foolish enough to try to push that through over my objections, I'll use my last dime to fight you in court."

As John Baron struggled to accept the thought of his own children's betrayal, Gillian tried wrapping her own mind around Bryce's news—he was going to be as outlandishly wealthy as he'd always promised her. And he'd done it on his own terms. Without her at his side.

Gillian couldn't help but admire him for that. In spite of the personal tragedy that had derailed their marriage, Bryce had never lost sight of his dream. She was only sorry she hadn't been there to share in his success.

"I'm proud of you," she said.

"Me, too. Damned proud," her father added.

His Adam's apple bobbed up and down as he struggled to keep his emotions under control.

"But that doesn't change my offer," John continued. "A young man as ambitious as you doesn't want to retire. What'll you do with yourself? You're not the type to be content filling your days with golf and endless travel. If you want to take this ranch in a new direction, I'd like to think I'm not so old that I can't change."

The brightness in her father's eyes told Gillian that he wanted Bryce to accept his offer not just for her sake but also for his own. The two of them shared a rare respect that existed well beyond their common interest in her.

"It's tempting," Bryce admitted. "But as Gillian pointed out, we've both got our own lives to live. I intend to relax and take a good long while off before making any decisions about what to do with the rest of my life. I've been thinking about starting up another business, one that allows a better balance between my professional and personal life. As much as I once loved your daughter and desperately wanted things to work out at one time, we could never heal our marriage when family members—" he glared at Rose and Stella "—kept tearing us apart. I've got to tell you, sir, I don't see that changing anytime soon."

Neither did Gillian. When her sisters didn't bother denying the charge, Bryce continued philosophically.

"There's a good woman waiting for me back in

Cheyenne, and I made a promise to a little boy I can't disappoint. I'm pretty sure the only thing more foolish than trying to start over with Gillian is denying myself the possibility of any future happiness with someone else."

The defeated look that settled into her father's features reminded Gillian of old Padre just waiting for someone to put him out of his misery. And made her wonder if he really hadn't intended for her and Bryce to reunite all along.

Twelve

Whether the tears stinging Gillian's eyes were from regret or resentment, she wasn't sure. Only one thing was certain—not only did Bryce not need her family's money nor want their most prized possession, the ranch, he didn't need or want *her*.

In spite of all the progress they'd made in resolving their differences, Gillian had to face the fact that he truly was over her. Having just assured everyone in the room that reconciliation wasn't in the cards, she wondered why she felt so betrayed. After all, she was the one who had initiated divorce in the first place. And she couldn't claim ignorance about Vi and her little boy being a part of Bryce's life before she had attempted to seduce him last night, either.

Gillian winced to see her father looking so defeated.

When had he gotten so old and frail? Who will watch out for him if not me?

Certainly neither Stella nor Rose. They looked so obviously relieved that Bryce wasn't interested in their father's money, Gillian couldn't help but feel ashamed of them.

Unlike her sisters, Gillian wouldn't simply tell her father whatever he wanted to hear in hopes of earning his favor. She would be there for him when he needed her—just as he'd been for her since the day she'd been born.

Lately she'd been battling a growing sense of dissatisfaction with putting in limitless hours at work just so she could avoid any kind of social life at all. Returning home was a poignant reminder of what was really important in her life, and it wasn't making a name for herself in an industry that measured people's worth by their credit rating. Nor making lots of money for some stranger to invest on her behalf because she was, quite frankly, too tired and busy to enjoy it.

A myriad of terrible images played in her head: her father falling, lying on the floor unable to reach the phone to call for help; sitting in a nursing home alone; his funeral on a cold and windy day.

Standing in the midst of her dysfunctional family and faced with the reality that Bryce wasn't about to rush to the rescue, it became suddenly clear to Gillian what had to be done.

"I'll do it," she said.

Rose looked perplexed. "Do what?"

"Move back home and help Dad take care of the ranch."

Bryce was shocked. He shook his head in disgust as Gillian's sisters halfheartedly tried to talk her out of giving up the career she'd worked so hard to establish. They were frustrated that their plans for immediately taking over their father's assets had fallen through, and Gillian's offer to take him completely out of the picture opened the door to further machinations on their part.

"Are you sure you want to do that?" Stella asked.

Bryce couldn't keep from adding his thoughts on the matter. "I suggest you think long and hard about giving up your professional life—"

"Just to sacrifice your own life for somebody who has already lived most of his," John finished, although clearly moved by the selflessness of his youngest daughter's decision. "You have no idea how much your offer means to me, but Bryce is right. That's too much to ask of one person alone."

Those words made Bryce feel suddenly small. He

hated to let down the old man. Although his immediate plans were to take a long, well-deserved rest pending the sale of his business, he couldn't deny that the thought of turning Moon Cussers into something extraordinary was intriguing.

When he looked at Gillian, he couldn't help but think of the night before. He'd never wanted to hurt her, but he could tell that she was taking his words to John hard despite the smile on her face.

"Nobody needs to feel like I'm giving up anything that I don't want to," she said. "The allure of a full-time career is fading, and this opportunity gives me a chance to do something meaningful with my life—like being where I'm needed most."

She turned to address her father specifically.

"There isn't any place I'd rather be than here with you, Dad. If you're willing to let me help you and the ranch without including Bryce in the package, I'll give notice as soon as I get back to Cheyenne and start putting things in order. But before I do, I want your assurance that you won't second-guess my decisions."

"You have my word," he promised. Tears clouded his eyes as he opened his arms to her.

Bryce had never heard the old man sob before. All at once he went from feeling pity for Gillian to feeling jealous of her. Once again he felt like an outsider looking in. His impending fortune meant little when compared to the love between Gillian and her father. He thought he would derive more satisfaction from breaking the news of his extraordinary success to the women who had helped destroy his marriage.

"This is wonderful news," Rose squeaked, rushing over to throw her arms around them both.

Bryce looked on skeptically as Stella joined in their family hug. As long as their inheritance remained intact for the time being, he doubted whether Gillian's sisters could care less about the sacrifice she was making on their behalf. After he was long gone, he supposed they would try to bully their sweet little sister into doing whatever they wanted.

He wasn't sure how successful they would be in that endeavor. Gillian wasn't the same naive little girl he'd married once upon a time nor the easy pushover Stella and Rose had manipulated in the past.

When he found it at last, Bryce's voice was rough around the edges. "I'll be leaving bright and early tomorrow, but I don't want you to think I'm abandoning you, John. I'll only be a phone call away. I'll continue to be involved in your affairs for as long as you want me to be."

Stella surprised him by assuming the unlikely role of peacemaker instead of taking exception to that remark as he would have expected.

"Now that everything's settled," she said, "what

do you say we have an old-fashioned Christmas like those we had when Mom was here? Rose and I brought along as many presents as we could pack on a snowmobile."

Rose's voice took on a nostalgic note. "A real Christmas dinner just like Mom used to make...."

"Turkey with all the trimmings," Stella continued.

"With pumpkin and pecan pie for dessert," Rose said excitedly.

"With fresh whipped cream..."

Listening to them reminisce reminded Bryce of all that had been missing from his own childhood. Accompanying his parents on a cruise now couldn't make up for all the sad holidays he'd spent as a kid, disappointed when Santa brought him socks, underwear and serviceable jeans instead of anything as extravagant as a new bike. Although he and his parents tried to get together on occasion, they would never be a real, loving family like the Barons, whose roots sunk so deeply into Red Rock Canyon that their blood was mixed into the soil for eternity. Despite his constant bickering with Stella and Rose, Bryce knew they loved Gillian and their father.

The next thing Bryce knew, he and John were being shooed out of the kitchen and into the living room with instructions to stay away while the women prepared a mouthwatering meal guaranteed to fulfill their every fantasy. Over the sounds of chitchat and laughter in the next room, the men relaxed in front of the television to watch a football game. Bryce had forgotten how much fun the Baron sisters could have when they all got together. They might be bossy, intrusive and opinionated, but they also shared a special bond that he couldn't help envying. He supposed it was only natural that Gillian's sisters felt threatened when she'd married a nobody from outside their tight circle of friends. A nobody with little more in his pockets at the time than dreams.

Dinner was a banquet that delighted all the senses at once. Since there hadn't been time to thaw and cook an entire turkey, a succulent ham decked with pineapple and drizzled with honey served as the main course. Cheesy scalloped potatoes, steamed asparagus topped with hollandaise sauce and flaky biscuits baked to a light, golden hue were presented on the floral blue china that Virginia Baron had saved for special occasions. For dessert, they had a decadent pecan pie piled high with whipped cream.

After shamelessly stuffing themselves, Gillian looked at her sisters. "I already mailed my Christmas presents to you. I hope you got them before you took off. If I'd known you were coming, I would have mailed them here instead."

Sheepishly Rose admitted to opening her gift the instant she'd received it rather than waiting for Christmas Day. "I love the cut-glass vase you sent me. It matches my pattern perfectly," she gushed.

Stella had gotten her present as well but, a stickler for tradition, she had waited to open it. She thanked Gillian in advance, then directed everyone to take a seat around the Christmas tree and presented her father with an exquisitely wrapped package. Inside was a gold Rolex.

"It's far too extravagant," John protested, confirming her assumption that it was just the kind of luxury he'd never buy for himself.

A snide remark popped into Bryce's mind about Stella using it to mark time until she tried collecting early on her inheritance again. He refrained, however, since there was no good reason to ruin the tentative truce they'd established at the holiest time of the year.

"Now I'm embarrassed to give you the flannel shirts I special ordered for you, Dad—even if you do desperately need some new ones," Gillian said, appreciatively eyeing the Rolex.

"Your coming to live here with me is the best present I could ever hope for," he assured her.

Something grabbed Bryce in the chest—hard—and refused let go of him. Until that very moment, he hadn't realized how deeply he longed to take back his old life the way Gillian was.

He drew a small nickel-plated, ivory-handled revolver out of his pocket and presented it to Gillian's father.

"I brought you something, too, John" he said. "Sorry I didn't get around to wrapping it."

The old man accepted the revolver reverently and examined it at length.

"A Colt dating back to the 1800s!" he exclaimed, reluctantly handing it back. "I'm afraid I can't accept something this expensive."

"You'll hurt my feelings if you don't," Bryce told him.

"Then thank you," he said, extending a hand in friendship. "It's the perfect piece to add to my collection."

Seeing the pride and happiness on his old friend's face was one of the best gifts Bryce could have received that Christmas.

Gillian swallowed against the emotion clogging her throat, wishing that her relationship with Bryce had been as uncomplicated as his with her father. She wished there was a way to hide the last present she had under the tree without drawing attention to the act. She didn't want her sisters reading anything more into that gift than was intended when she'd bought it as a token of appreciation for Bryce coming here with her on such short notice.

Rose got a funny look on her face as she withdrew the small, ornately wrapped package from under the tree and read the gift tag aloud. She passed it to Bryce with all the temerity of a spy handing over a package of Grade A plutonium.

He looked just as surprised. Beneath the foil wrapping was an expensive business card holder. Carved from elk antler, it boasted a brass insert upon which an image of a grizzly was etched.

"If you're going to be a bear…" Gillian said, recalling his old motto.

"You might as well be a grizzly," Bryce finished for her.

They exchanged a look that made everyone else disappear. The room grew hotter as they gazed at each other.

"I feel silly," she said. "Had I known you were selling your business, I never would have bought it," she explained feebly.

Bryce leaned in, his eyes never leaving hers. "I love it."

Those words were warmed by a gracious smile. Gillian could hear the thrum of blood rushing through her veins. Every nerve in her body was aware of the man sitting next to her.

"I'd better call Vi, wish her a happy Christmas Eve and assure her I'll do my damnedest to get home tomorrow," he said, rising to his feet and running for the safe haven of the next room.

Gillian felt torn between gratitude to the woman for loaning out her fiancée over the holidays and jealousy so ferocious it clawed at her guts. She pasted a false smile on her face only to realize that her family was either deliberately avoiding making eye contact with her, or studying her with expressions of pity.

When Bryce returned a little while later, he looked surprised to see Rose and Stella packing up their things.

"It was hard enough getting here in daylight. I hate to think about navigating the trail in the dark," Stella explained. "And I don't want to risk waiting around until another avalanche traps us here indefinitely."

Once her mind was made up, arguing with the woman was useless. So despite her father's insistence that they remain and Rose's suggestion that they at least wait until morning and leave with Bryce, they were soon saying their goodbyes. John kissed them farewell and asked them to keep in touch more often. Stella even managed a polite "Merry Christmas" to Bryce before heading to her snowmobile with all the determination of a general deploying her troops. Mumbling under her breath, Rose followed behind.

Gillian was honestly sorry to see them go. She

stood in the doorway a long time, watching their re-
treating figures cut a path through the snow. The roar
of their snowmobiles died away before her father
saw fit to close the door on the cold air that rushed
to fill the house with their absence.

Thirteen

Once they were all settled in the living room, John suggested a game of cards. They spent the next couple of hours filling the room with the sounds of good-natured ribbing that brought back childhood recollections for Gillian as crystalline as the snow that began falling softly outside.

"This is the best Christmas I can remember since your mother passed away," her father said at one point.

She agreed.

It was nice to laugh and enjoy familiar company again. To be sure, it had been too long since Gillian had asked herself what she wanted out of life—

beyond tamping down any memory that might bring back the pain she'd felt after Bonnie's death. Unfortunately, she'd also buried any memories with the power to heal the hurt, as well.

She knew Bryce thought she was crazy for giving up a successful career to return to a life she'd left so long ago. But the funny thing was she hadn't felt more certain about anything since Bonnie had died and left her so unsure about absolutely everything.

Gillian wasn't about to be dissuaded from that gut feeling by anything as mundane as logic. She'd listened to her head too much since that horrible day, and all she'd managed to do was forget how to live.

She leaned over the edge of the table to kiss her father on his roughened cheek. In spite of his deteriorating health, the hug she received in return was strong enough to crush her bones but luckily not the heart she'd so recently taken out of storage. She was still having trouble dismissing the nagging suspicion that her father had exaggerated his condition in hopes of bringing her back together with the son-in-law for whom he still cared so deeply.

Too bad it didn't work, she thought wistfully.

Returning her attention to the card game, she grinned when she noticed her hand. "Gin!" she yelled.

Slapping his cards down on the table, John glared at her.

"Do I really want somebody running this place who'd cheat her own father at cards?"

Since Bryce had flatly turned down her father's request to run his empire, Gillian wondered if he wasn't really worried about how she would manage a place of this size alone.

"I don't know. Do you?"

Her father's expression grew suddenly pensive as he gave the question some thought.

"Only if it's what you really want, Gillian. I don't want you giving up your life to move home. Taking care of an old coot like me isn't exactly the future your mother and I envisioned for our baby girl."

Gillian smiled as she attempted to explain her reasoning to everyone in the room. Including herself.

"Some of the dreams we have for our children are taken out of our hands," she said, fighting back a sense of melancholy. "And some are miraculously given back when we least expect it. I loved Bonnie fiercely, but I don't think she would have wanted me to tie myself to a stressful job and lock myself away in an empty apartment. Yes, I admit I was hesitant to come home, but it's been the smartest decision I've made since she passed. It's made me remember how important it is to hold on to the people we love for as long as we can."

Looking at Bryce through a sheen of tears, Gillian

wished she could make him understand how sorry she was about the part she'd played in everything that had gone wrong between them.

Her explanation seemed to satisfy her father, if not her ex-husband. "It's good to know that somebody loves me for more than money alone," he said.

Dropping her gaze, Gillian found she couldn't look her father in the eye. She felt terrible for the way her sisters had acted and hoped that, in time, she could help her family heal.

Turning to Bryce, he added, "The richer you become, you'll find the more that will mean to you."

That said, he excused himself from the game and shuffled down to his room, using the wall for leverage the entire way.

In the distance, the lonely refrain of a coyote's song echoed off the cliffs surrounding the ranch on three sides. The sound caused an unexpected sense of panic to well up in Bryce's chest at the thought of leaving Gillian and her father all alone to fend for themselves. Not the type given to "analysis paralysis," he rose impatiently to his feet, wishing there were some easy way to put his worries behind him.

"I'll be leaving first thing tomorrow morning. With your father's affairs in order and your mind made up about taking over the responsibility of the ranch, there's really no reason for me to hang around any longer."

"There's no hurry," Gillian said.

"There is if I want to make it back by midnight Christmas Day and I told Robbie that I'd take him to a ball game in Denver. I don't intend to break another promise to someone I love for as long as I live."

He was thinking about his promise to always be there for Gillian, the one he'd broken the day his baby had died and Gillian had been so alone she'd nearly gone out of her mind waiting for him to arrive.

Bryce pushed aside those heavy memories to focus on something more affirming. "Before I go, I have something for you, too."

"You didn't have to do that," Gillian protested.

She followed meekly as he led the way into the other room and sat her down in front of the Christmas tree. The look on her pretty face as she watched him rustling around in the tree's branches made Bryce glad that he had acted on impulse. With a flourish, he extracted a tiny envelope with her name neatly written on it. He shook off a couple of strands of tinsel that were clinging to his sweater before handing it to her. Inside she found a gilt business card with the name Carl Hartman embossed upon it. He was one of her favorite artists, a local who had made quite a name for himself on the prestigious Jackson

Hole art scene. The commission on one of his paintings alone was often as much as Gillian made selling a house in Cheyenne.

"Before our flight, I sent Carl a copy of the photograph of Bonnie in my bedroom and asked him to duplicate it in oil for you. He'll have it done in a couple of months."

His voice suddenly broke as he took her hand in his. "It's dedicated to all that we once shared, not everything we lost."

Seeing her dab at her eyes with the back of her hand, he could barely refrain from wrapping his arms around her. Seized by emotions beyond his control, he felt his heart trip over the possibility that they could finally let the past go and embrace it at the same time.

"You have no idea how much this means to me," Gillian said, truly touched by Bryce's thoughtful gift.

Not so long ago she questioned whether she could live with such a poignant image openly displayed in her home for fear that the memories evoked would incapacitate her. Today a ray of sunshine pierced the shroud of darkness that had been holding her hostage for so very long. She'd come full circle returning home and she was now able to let go of past hurts and wanted to share her newfound sense of redemption with the man she'd lashed out at during a time when they should have been offering each other comfort.

"I-it was wrong of me to blame you for not being there when Bonnie…"

Swallowing hard, Gillian steadied herself by laying a hand on Bryce's chest. The beat of his heart against her palm stirred old emotions.

"No one can predict SIDS," she said, quoting from the stacks of materials she'd waded through after the tragic turn of events that changed their lives. "You couldn't have possibly known what was going to happen any more than I could. No one could. Otherwise you would have been there. I know that nothing could have kept you away. I hope you can forgive me for ever insinuating otherwise."

Bryce sucked a breath into his lungs, breaking the silence that followed her apology.

"That you can ask *me* to forgive *you*…" His voice cracked like icicles driven into frozen ground by the force of their own weight. "I'm the one who desperately needs you to forgive me."

Gillian tilted her face toward the twinkling Christmas lights and blinked back the tears welling to the surface. Raw with need, she let him take her into his arms. Lust finally sheared away the last of his restraint as he muttered an unintelligible oath and claimed her mouth.

Hot, wild and wet, his kisses awakened a feral response in Gillian. Linking her arms around his neck, she offered herself to him as the final present under the tree. Although she could not hope to have him for more than one night, she silently vowed that if he would just give her one more chance, she would somehow find the courage to make her days worthwhile, if not truly enchanted by a more lasting love, when he was gone.

Even if it meant sustaining herself on memories alone.

Seeing herself reflected in his eyes, which were blazing with desire, Gillian never felt more beautiful. She reveled in the warmth of his skin against her hands as she drew his sweater slowly over his head. A moment later she was resting her head against the wide expanse of his bare chest. Passion sizzled as they surrendered to their desires.

"Gillian," he murmured into her hair.

The huskiness of Bryce's voice was both rough and tender. She tore her jersey over her head, then stood still in the glowing light of the fireplace and allowed him to admire her breasts as she reached behind her back and divested herself of the scrap of lace that restrained them.

They discarded the rest of their clothes in a frenzy without regard to where they fell. Their urgency to be together defied the logic that compelled Bryce to take a condom from his wallet. Considering that they'd been unable to conceive a child for months after Bonnie's death, Gillian thought it a waste of time. He gave her no chance to voice any objections, though, and a moment later she was begging him to take her.

Drawing her to her knees on the carpet, he asked in a strangled voice, "Are you sure about this?"

Gillian didn't have the courage to ask him the same question.

"I want you in me now," she said instead.

That throaty command rendered foreplay unnecessary. Gillian pushed him onto his back, climbed on top of him and, without stopping to consider his impressive size, braced herself by clutching his shoulders and claiming him all at once.

Groaning, Bryce took her by the hips and guided her movements in a way that maximized his pleasure while simultaneously intensifying hers.

Throwing her head back, she gasped as their bodies, their souls became one. Gillian moaned. Called out Bryce's name. And said a little prayer to commit every loving detail of this night to memory.

Tangling his hands in her hair, Bryce drew her down to him and kissed her. Those slow, measured kisses matched the rhythm of his driving force. When she made the slightest move to change position, he merely tightened his grip.

"I'll let you go when I'm good and ready," he

growled, keeping the hot, delicious slickness of his mouth centered on hers.

He disentangled his fingers from her hair and focused on caressing the silky-smooth length of her body. Tenderly he dawdled over the small of her back before moving onto her rib cage and stopping to explore the swell of her breasts pressed against his chest. Gillian whimpered into the hollow of his collarbone.

Bryce would have none of it.

"I want you to look at the man who's making love to you," he commanded, thrusting into her with ragged, shuddering breaths.

Gillian did as she was told. Digging her fingernails into his shoulders, a moment later she crested on an orgasm that took her out of her body. Multicolored lights exploded behind her eyes as Bryce joined her someplace suspended between heaven and earth.

His whole body shuddered as he poured himself into her. Cherishing the beat of his heart beneath her own, Gillian held him tightly to keep him exactly where she wanted for as long as she wanted.

Chests heaving, they clung to each other beneath the glimmering Christmas lights and the watchful eyes of the angel standing guard atop the tree. Their tangled limbs and a blazing fire kept the cold away until they could no longer ignore that either a blanket or a change of rooms was necessary.

"Want to take a shower with me?" Bryce asked, rubbing away the shivers rising along her bare arms.

Having already enjoyed her sin so completely, Gillian saw no point in forgoing the pleasures of the flesh before the morning sun dictated that she had to. Surely there would be time for regrets and recriminations later.

She held out her hands. "Help me up."

Bryce pulled her to her feet as if she were made of nothing more than fluff. Together, they padded up the stairs naked to the master bathroom where he turned on the water and adjusted it to the right temperature before they both stepped inside.

Parts of Gillian that were sore from their lovemaking welcomed the gentle massage of water. Dizzy from the aftereffects, she leaned against Bryce's strong, hard body and willed the warm water to wash away her guilt.

Was there anything worse than discovering that she was still in love with the man she'd divorced?

Perhaps only the terrible knowledge that he no longer felt the same way about her.

Refusing to belabor that which she could not change, Gillian proceeded to soap Bryce's back with great tenderness. She rubbed shampoo into his hair and massaged his head gently with her fingernails, making him so content he was almost purring.

"Turnabout's fair play," he said, intent on returning the favor.

He proceeded to soap her breasts, sore from the demanding caresses they'd received earlier, only to inflict more sweet abuse upon them with his mouth, suckling her beneath the warm, running water. Gillian pressed her back against the wall, making no move to escape when he followed the brazen act by dropping to his knees in front of her. She gave in to more than just the guttural sounds welling up inside her and opened herself to everything he had to offer. The delicious pressure of his tongue made her explode into a million flickering fragments of light.

They had to have been in the shower a long time for the hot water heater gave out. Shutting off the tepid stream, Bryce helped Gillian out of the stall and offered to dry her off with a big, white fluffy towel.

"I can barely stand up," she admitted, grateful that he had the strength to carry her down the hall to his bedroom.

They spent the rest of the night in a sturdy hand-carved bed, wrapped in nothing more than clean sheets and each other's loving arms. Tomorrow Gillian knew that life would fall back into place as if nothing more than civil words had passed between them. But knowing she had a lifetime left to rue the past, she chose to enjoy this one magical night.

Sex with Bryce had always been wonderful, but by the end of their marriage, they'd deliberately turned their backs on each other in the bed they'd shared, unable to reach out to the other. After tonight Gillian didn't know how she could ever go back to sleeping alone.

Smiling past her tears, she was rewarded with an encore of kisses and caresses that resurrected something inside her that felt too much like hope.

Fourteen

"I could never stop loving you, no matter how hard I tried," Gillian whispered in the dark.

The words rocketed into Bryce's brain like a heat-seeking missile, destroying any preconceptions he might have had about the night being a farewell to the past before they finally went their own separate ways once and for all.

He couldn't quite wrap his mind around the possibility that Gillian still loved him.

Had never actually stopped loving him.

Moved by the raw emotion shimmering in her soft

violet eyes, his whole being cried out with the realization that he loved her, too.

But he could never admit it.

Studying her silhouette in the moonlight, he was certain that there wasn't a single molecule in her body that he didn't cherish. Awake or asleep Gillian was the most beautiful woman he'd ever known. That didn't mean there could ever be anything between them again, though. After the way their marriage had crumbled, he couldn't see how something permanent could be built out of the rubble.

One maddening little phrase kept repeating itself over and over in his head. *Too little, too late.*

In the silence following Gillian's sex-induced admission, Bryce heard her stop breathing. Reaching over to place his hand over her heart, he found her skin still damp from their lovemaking.

She directed her gaze to the base of his throat. "I'm so sorry I hurt you," she mumbled. "So damned sorry."

In response to the shudder that ran the length of her body, Bryce wrapped his arms tightly around her. He couldn't let her go like this, racing for the safety of her own bed, leaving him to suffer in the silence of what he could not bring himself to say.

"I'm also sorry for what I just told you," she added in a hoarse whisper. "Given where you are in your life right now, it was wrong of me."

Bryce could love her no less for gathering her pride about her like the sheet she drew over her breasts.

"No, you probably shouldn't have," he conceded. "Any more than I should have ever made love to you. For God's sake, Gillian, I'm *engaged* to another woman! Someone who put her trust in me when I promised that there was nothing left between you and me."

"Vi doesn't have to know." Her voice was flat.

For the second time in less than five minutes, Bryce couldn't believe his ears.

"Is that how little you think of me?" he demanded, letting her go roughly. "Do you really think I could marry another woman with a lie of that magnitude hanging over my head? We made a mistake, Gillian. You know that as well as I do, and Vi needs to know."

"The truth isn't going to absolve you, and it won't do anything but hurt her, either," Gillian said evenly in response to his rising voice. "Maybe it wasn't right, but we were two lonely people who hurt each other in the past and somehow managed to put that hurt behind them for a single night. That isn't the worst thing that could ever happen."

Bryce raked his fingers through his hair in exasperation. He wasn't proud of what he'd done and couldn't imagine living with the ugly lie for the rest of his life. But that wasn't to say that Gillian might not be right about there being no need to hurt Vi just to assuage his sense of guilt, either.

Gentle fingers stroked the lines of his jaw darkened by a day's growth of stubble. "If we ever hope to find happiness again, we have to forgive each other for being human," Gillian said soothingly.

Her unexpected kindness made Bryce feel worse than had she hurled hateful accusations in his face. Or threatened to tell Vi herself. At the same time, he knew he couldn't hide this from Vi. He already had one failed marriage; he didn't need to add another one to the list.

"That's easy for you to say," he said. "You aren't the one who betrayed your fiancée. You're not the one who has to face a little boy who's already started calling you Daddy."

Gillian couldn't bear to hear another word. She understood how a man's pride could get in the way of his heart, but when she was lying naked in bed with him, the last thing she wanted to hear about was another woman.

Or her darling, healthy child.

Considering their history, Gillian shouldn't have been so surprised to have Bryce take a great big bite out of her heart before offering it back to her on the silver platter she'd polished to a sheen with the last shreds of her pride. She couldn't believe she'd been so stupid as to expose her vulnerabilities to the very man she'd been doing her best to forget. She'd been a fool for thinking he could ever feel anything more for her than pure and simple lust.

Gillian rolled to the side of the bed and sat up, protectively wrapping her arms around herself.

"You're right. I don't have to face anyone but myself in the mirror. Unlike you, I haven't found anyone who's even come close to replacing the void in my life. The best I can do right now is cling to my family. So if you're looking for me to apologize for seducing you tonight, you might as well forget it!"

The hard note in her voice was intended to bring the conversation to a close, but Bryce snaked an arm around her waist and tried pulling her back into the warmth of his bed.

"It isn't exactly fair to say that you seduced me," he admitted.

That Gillian was unsuccessful in pulling away from his embrace wasn't from lack of trying. Both were panting hard by the time Bryce pinned her down with his superior strength. She groaned in protest when, in spite of her anger, desire once again flared in the pit of her belly.

"Would you stop fighting me for a minute and listen to what I have to say?"

At the moment, Gillian would have agreed to

anything just so long as he let her go. Forcing herself to lie still, she grudgingly consented to hear him out.

"I'd have to be blind not to notice how uncomfortable you get whenever the subject of Robbie comes up. I want you to know that I wasn't drawn to Vi just because I wanted to be a father to her little boy. Surely you know that nobody will ever replace Bonnie in my life. Nobody."

He repeated the word with such conviction that it was hard for her to doubt the depth of his sincerity. Gillian felt herself relax slightly in his arms.

"Just like nobody is ever going to be able to replace what we once had together. But as tempting as it might be to give our relationship another try, I just don't see us going down that path again. After all, what's really changed to make things turn out any different this time?"

Me! she longed to tell him. *I've changed. And I'd do anything to get you back.*

Pride warned her to remain quiet however. Indiscriminately throwing words like those around would just reopen wounds that were only now beginning to heal.

"Your sisters still don't trust me," Bryce reminded her. "Just the thought of us being alone sent them racing to our doorstep at the speed of light. I don't ever see an end to their meddling."

Neither did Gillian, but having grown up a whole lot over the past couple of years, she knew things would be different when it came to Bryce. Never again would she seek outside advice in matters of the heart.

"Whatever they might have told you," Bryce continued earnestly, "it's important that you know I don't think you any less a woman just because we didn't conceive another child together."

He released his grip on her but kept her pinned with a soul-searching gaze.

"Looking back, I think we both just tried too hard after we lost Bonnie. It all became so clinical. In bed. In our marriage. In what we allowed ourselves to say—and not to say—to each other."

Gillian lay perfectly still. If only they had somehow found the courage to have this conversation years ago, there was a good possibility they would still be married today.

"Sweetheart," Bryce said, seemingly oblivious to how that simple endearment moved her. "I can't stand the thought of you living the rest of your life under the assumption that God is punishing you for something either of us did or didn't do. I know it's hard to understand, but sometimes bad things happen to good people for no reason."

The back of Gillian's eyelids stung as she blinked back tears. Logically, it was easy enough to accept that she might never have children again and that that didn't mean she was somehow defective. Emotionally, however, that truth was harder to believe whenever somebody posed a thoughtless question about why she didn't just have another child to replace the one they'd lost. As if it was as easy as going to the pound to pick out a puppy after burying the family pet.

"I want you to know that I would gladly give up every minute spent building my career to buy back time with our precious little girl. I would toss away every cent I have for a second chance just to make things right between us."

"Shh…" she whispered, putting a finger to his lips, which were swollen from kissing her, and trying to stop the words pouring forth from the depth of his soul. They were solace to her wounded spirit, and she would carry those sweet words to her grave.

Gillian could no longer deny that Bryce was the one thing she wanted more than anything else in this world. More than house or home or security or even another child—although that longing would surely remain with her till the end of her days.

Although she knew better than to give herself over to wishful thinking, she decided that tomorrow was soon enough to face reality. Tonight she intended to rewrite destiny—if only in her mind.

Torn between desperately wanting this man and needing to let him go graciously, Gillian spent the rest of the evening committing to memory every loving detail of a night that would have to last her a lifetime: his musky, masculine scent; the salty taste of his skin; the ripple of muscles beneath her fingers; the curve of his lips brushing against her own; the texture of his hair; and the rise and fall of each and every breath he took.

At dawn when Gillian woke to the muted sound of Bryce's conversation with Vi on the phone in the next room, she was not at all surprised that it was followed shortly thereafter by the roar of a snowmobile pulling out of the driveway and heading in the direction of the distant horizon.

Fifteen

Since the ground was too hard to dig a grave by hand, Dusty used a backhoe to turn over a little piece of earth in the aspen grove behind the house. He looked relieved when Gillian thanked him for all his help and told him that she would take care of the rest herself.

"It's the least I can do for such a devoted companion," she explained.

Tamping down the last shovelful of dirt, she said her goodbyes to the one friend who'd never failed to protect her without thought to his own safety or to offer his love unconditionally. Claiming he could no longer bear the cold weather, her father shed his tears in private and watched out the window as his daughter got down on her knees in the snow to say a prayer that everyone she loved might someday go to heaven as easily as Padre had drifted away in his sleep.

Although she hadn't cried since Bryce had taken off without a backward glance, it was hard fighting back the sniffles on such a sad occasion. Nearby the river gurgled beneath layers of frozen ice, hinting of the spring thaw that was sure to come, although no one could predict exactly when. Thoughts of green shoots lying dormant under the snowpack renewed in her a sense of hope that had disappeared Christmas morning on the back of a snowmobile. If the world could miraculously manage to rebirth itself every year, Gillian liked to think that it wasn't altogether inconceivable to imagine the human spirit doing likewise.

To that end, she imagined Vi had forgiven Bryce for his little "indiscretion" on one condition—that he promise never speak to his ex-wife ever again.

It was not an altogether unreasonable request.

Still, thoughts of the happy couple all cozied up on a couch with Robbie playing happily at their feet were enough to make Gillian physically sick to her stomach. And unwelcome images of them in bed together kept coming between her and a good night's sleep. It was little wonder she felt so tired all the time. Or that she'd skipped a period.

It was easy enough to blame her fatigue and nausea on the pressure of quitting her job, packing up her things and moving back home all within such a short time frame. Not to mention the incredible amount of work involved in running a ranch the size of this one, especially when she was in the midst of taking it in an entirely different direction. One that included getting more help for Dusty and hiring an on-site caretaker to see to her father's daily needs so that she could attend to more pressing matters, such as laying the groundwork for Moon Cussers to become a premier destination spot for some of the finest trout fishing and hunting in the nation.

However, the following month, when she fainted in the barn and came to with hay sticking out of her hair, Gillian could no longer dismiss the sudden changes to her health as merely stress-related. She'd already dismissed the possibility of pregnancy. Since she'd been unable to conceive when she and Bryce had tried so hard to make a baby, it seemed highly improbable he would impregnate her when he'd used a condom.

Worried that some other medical cause was the root of her problems, Gillian was glad that she'd carried her insurance from work forward until her private coverage kicked in. She wondered if her sisters would appreciate the irony of her falling ill so soon after volunteering to nurse their father back to full health.

Picking herself up off the barn floor, she dusted herself off, thinking there was little reason to share her concerns with anyone else until she'd given a doctor a chance to run some tests.

Stepping out from under the shade of the barn, she paused, scarcely able to remember a time when the aspen trees had budded so soon. She hoped a wet snow didn't bend their supple limbs to the breaking point. If they showed but a little of her father's resiliency, they would probably be just fine. The instant she'd moved back home and assumed the burden of running the ranch, he seemed to shrug the years off his rounded shoulders.

Beneath a blue sky that had no beginning or end, Gillian suddenly was filled with an inexplicable sense that her own little girl might be sending a gift from beyond. Hopefully it was one that would make Gillian remember that miracles could happen and that she would have her own soon.

A little less than a week later, Gillian prepared for whatever the doctor had to tell her. Dr. Schuler greeted her with a great big smile as he stepped through the door.

"Happy news for Valentine's Day," he announced jovially. "You're going to have a baby."

Those words bounced off the office walls and reverberated through the decorative string of shiny red hearts taped to the front of his desk.

"I'm afraid that you've got your holidays mixed up," she said, giving her old family friend a look that let him know she didn't find his odd sense of humor a bit funny. "April Fools' Day is in two months."

His responding laughter did little to dispel her incredulity as he pulled out a pad and began writing prescriptions for prenatal care vitamins and supplements.

Still in shock, she wondered whether Bryce even realized the condom they'd used had been faulty. She doubted it. Likely he would be just as bowled over by the news of her pregnancy as she was. Nonetheless, Gillian didn't want to tell him the news until she was comfortable with it herself. What point was there in throwing everybody into a dither until the critical third month had passed and the threat of a miscarriage was greatly reduced anyway?

Bryce needed some crazy, pregnant woman hanging on to him like he needed a rock tied around his neck. Especially when the rock was his ex-wife. Besides, he was already committed to marrying someone else.

Gillian had no desire to bind him to her through a misplaced sense of duty or guilt, but knowing how passionate he felt about his own father's lackadaisical style of parenting, she doubted Bryce would ever willingly opt for absentee fathering himself. And that would jeopardize the wonderful life he was building with Vi and Robbie, neither of whom should be punished for her poor judgment.

If her father suspected anything out of the ordinary as the days passed, he kept it to himself. He'd been treading lightly around his daughter ever since, in a hormone-induced fit, she'd accused him of master-minding the entire drama at Christmas to get her back together with Bryce.

He didn't deny it.

And, much to her surprise, Gillian discovered that she was no longer able to hold it against him.

Later that month, Gillian found herself back in the kitchen mixing up yet another pan of brownies. Putting a hand to her back, she stretched with the languid luxury of a cat looking for a sunny spot to take a little nap. Lately she just couldn't get her fill of chocolate. Or sauerkraut. Or the view of the Tetons out the window. Or the funny feeling that crept up on her and left a goofy smile on her face at odd times throughout the day.

In spite of the latest curveball she'd been thrown, Gillian was so much happier than she'd been just a year ago. Make no mistake about it—life was no-where near as perfect it had been once upon a time before heartbreak turned it upside down, but it was immeasurably better than those horrendous days following her divorce.

Understandably it was even harder for her to let go of Bryce now than before. She hadn't realized how often he would slip uninvited into her thoughts. A pair of geese waddling down a frozen riverbank made her long for her own wandering gander. The sound of an elk bugling in the timber made her wish she had someone to share a similar revered courtship ritual. Stars on a cloudless night brought *his* eyes to mind. And just then, the sound of the front doorbell sent her imagination into overdrive with silly images of a blond Adonis waiting for her on the porch holding out a bouquet of roses and a great big diamond—

"Would you mind getting that?" her father called from the bathroom.

Slipping the pan into the oven, Gillian gave the timer a cursory glance before padding into the living room. She wiped her hands on her apron before throwing open the front door. The reality of finding Bryce standing on the front porch was very different than she'd imagined it.

He didn't have any roses.

And he wasn't smiling.

High altitude had nothing to do with how difficult

it was forcing air into her lungs. Singed by a smoldering gaze, Gillian realized that loving this man at a distance was far safer than facing him up close and personal. The floor swayed beneath her feet. Grabbing the nearest wall to steady herself, she swallowed hard and summoned all of her lost composure.

Her hand self-consciously went to her hair. Since her new life didn't include a routine list of dates and the livestock paid no mind to her appearance, she'd adopted a simple look since moving back home. Her chic hairdo was growing out, and she'd barely bothered to put on a smidgen of lipstick and mascara earlier in the day.

Once Gillian managed to get her heart to start beating again, she stammered, "What are you doing here?"

"We need to talk."

Nodding mutely, she gestured for him to come inside, then hid her shaking hands in the deep pockets of her apron. She could think of no reason he would be here giving her such a hard, searching look unless…unless…

Unless her father was up to his old tricks, and he'd told Bryce that she was pregnant!

But that was impossible. How could that cagey old man have possibly guessed the truth? Had her insatiable cravings tipped him off? Her need for a nap every day? Or was it simple wishful thinking on his part?

In the time it took Bryce to divest himself of his heavy coat and take a seat on the couch, Gillian had worked herself into a terrible state wondering whether her father had somehow conned the information out of their longtime family physician. Whatever his suspicions, he had no right to meddle in her affairs.

Had he not chosen to lock himself in the bathroom, Gillian probably would have questioned him in front of a hostile eye witness.

"What do you want?" she asked, not bothering to sit down herself.

Bryce hadn't so much as cracked a smile since he'd arrived. His voice was as rough as his gaze was direct.

"I told Vi everything," he said.

Gillian's world skidded to a halt as she stood gaping at him in total disbelief. "Why in God's name would you do that?"

"Because it was the right thing to do, and you know it."

Her mind raced out of control as she imagined the worst-case scenarios coming from such an ill-advised confession.

"What did she say?"

"She was deeply hurt naturally. And she wanted to know if I still loved you."

It was the same question Gillian had been asking

herself ever since he'd driven away with her heart weeks ago. It was all she could do to refrain from demanding an answer herself.

"That's why I'm here," he explained evenly. "Because I couldn't look Vi in the eye and tell her that I'm *not* still in love with you. I'm here because since I left, nothing's been right. I'm more successful than I ever dreamed possible. I have more money than I can spend. And I'm miserable. I'm here because I want you to marry me."

When he finally smiled, Gillian blinked slowly as her heart performed a series of crazy acrobatic feats that would have left a cardiac surgeon shaking his head. Her knees failed her, and she sank down next to him on the couch.

The only thing stopping her from smothering him with kisses when he gathered her into his arms and crushed her to his chest was the terrible thought that his proposal might be motivated by news of her pregnancy and not a genuine desire to marry her for herself.

Gillian couldn't answer him unless she knew the truth. No matter how painful it might be.

"Does this have anything to do with my father spilling the beans?" she demanded. Righteous indignation held her chin up and kept the waver out of her voice.

"Why? Has something happened to John? Or is

there some problem with the ranch?" Bryce looked so genuinely worried that her fury lost some, though not all, of its storm.

"I'm not some pathetic charity case in need of pity, and I'd appreciate you telling that to my father and the ever-understanding Vi, too, for that matter."

Bryce held up both hands in surrender as his concern turned to confusion.

"I haven't spoken to John since I left here. And, just for the record, Vi wasn't all that understanding. But she's not the kind of woman who'd marry a man just to give her son a father. Especially not when he's in love with someone else."

If ever sweeter words were uttered, Gillian had yet to hear them. He didn't know about the baby, and he wasn't asking her to marry him out of some misplaced sense of obligation.

That wonderful revelation posed another quandary, though. How was she going to break the news to Bryce that he was going to be a father? How would he react to her keeping that a secret from him?

"What does John have to do with my being here anyway?" Bryce asked, looking at her directly.

"Nothing," she began when the timer went off in the kitchen. Grateful for any excuse to gather her wits about her, Gillian jumped to her feet.

"My brownies!" she said by way of explanation.

Not so easily distracted, Bryce pulled her back into the seat beside him. "Whatever you have in the oven can wait."

Gillian closed her eyes against the sunshine filtering into the room through the lace curtains. She hoped her omission wouldn't make him reconsider wanting to put a ring upon her finger. Things were definitely more complicated than that long ago day when she'd come home bursting with news that she was pregnant with Bonnie.

"We're going to have a baby," she blurted out in a raspy voice.

Bryce's stunned reaction confirmed that this was the first he'd heard about it. The temperature in the room dropped several degrees by the time he found his voice.

"Were you ever going to tell me?" he asked.

Gillian nodded her head. "After the third month. Or after you married Vi. Whichever came first."

Bryce's hoarse laugh was without humor.

Gillian reached out to cup his face with trembling fingers and did her best to explain herself.

"I didn't want to force you into a relationship if you wanted to be with someone else. I didn't want you to feel honor bound to ruin what you have with Vi and that little boy who already thinks of you as a father."

"I'll still be his friend," Bryce said fiercely. "I'll always be his friend."

If he thought she was going to be so ignorant as to argue with such pure loyalty, he was mistaken. She certainly wasn't going to take that away from him. Gillian felt bad for Robbie—and for his mother, too.

Bryce looked so deeply into her eyes that Gillian could actually feel his soul connecting with hers.

"That said, there's something that you should understand about me. In my whole life I've loved only one woman and I never want to lose her again. I can't think of anything more exciting than starting a new life with you and the new baby on the way."

He emphasized the point by pulling Gillian to him for a kiss that devoured the sigh on her lips and left her begging for more.

"Do you want me to get down on my knees?" he asked.

Gillian shook her head.

Blissfully happy, she didn't require such formalities. Or ask for any guarantees. She understood better than most that one day did not automatically entitle a person to another. Yet, in spite of that terrible knowledge, she refused to be a prisoner of fear or blame ever again. Not everyone was lucky enough to get a second chance at love—a chance to make life as perfect as was possible on a crazy, imperfect planet.

"That won't be necessary," she said, smiling softly. "I'll marry you. Next year, next week, tomorrow or right now if you want."

"It wouldn't be soon enough."

Bryce lowered his mouth to kiss her again only to draw away in surprise when a loud voice from the other room interrupted. "What's burning out there?"

"I hope it's your ears," Gillian called out.

Bryce laughed. "I can hardly wait to see the expression on your father's face when he hears he's going to be a grandpa again."

Standing up, Bryce offered a hand to the woman whom he'd never been able to let out of his heart. Just as the past had hurt so many people, the future was certain to fill the emptiness in many more lives than just their own. Gillian slipped her hand into his as they went to tell her father the good news together.

"I hope he has the decency to act surprised," she said with a wry little laugh.

* * * * *

Mediterranean NIGHTS™

*Sail aboard the luxurious Alexandra's Dream and
experience glamour, romance, mystery and revenge!*

Coming in October 2007...

AN AFFAIR TO REMEMBER

by
Karen Kendall

When Captain Nikolas Pappas first fell in love with
Helena Stamos, he was a penniless deckhand and she
was the daughter of a shipping magnate. But he's
never forgiven himself for the way he left her—and
fifteen years later, he's determined to win her back.

Though the attraction is still there, Helena is hesitant
to get involved. Nick left her once...what's to stop
him from doing it again?

Silhouette® Desire

There was only one man for the job—
an impossible-to-resist maverick
she knew she didn't dare fall for.

MAVERICK
(#1827)

BY *NEW YORK TIMES*
BESTSELLING AUTHOR
JOAN HOHL

"Will You Do It for One Million Dollars?"

Any other time, Tanner Wolfe would have balked at being
hired by a woman. Yet Brianna Stewart was desperate to
engage the infamous bounty hunter. The price was just
high enough to gain Tanner's interest…Brianna's beauty
definitely strong enough to keep it. But he wasn't about
to allow her to tag along on his mission. He worked
alone. Always had. Always would. However, he'd never
confronted a more determined client than Brianna. She
wasn't taking no for an answer—not about anything.

Perhaps a million-dollar bounty was not the only thing
this maverick was about to gain….

Look for MAVERICK

Available October 2007 wherever you buy books.

REQUEST YOUR FREE BOOKS!

2 FREE NOVELS PLUS 2 FREE GIFTS!

Passionate, Powerful, Provocative!

YES! Please send me 2 FREE Silhouette Desire® novels and my 2 FREE gifts. After receiving them, if I don't wish to receive any more books, I can return the shipping statement marked "cancel." If I don't cancel, I will receive 6 brand-new novels every month and be billed just $3.80 per book in the U.S., or $4.47 per book in Canada, plus 25¢ shipping and handling per book and applicable taxes, if any*. That's a savings of almost 15% off the cover price! I understand that accepting the 2 free books and gifts places me under no obligation to buy anything. I can always return a shipment and cancel at any time. Even if I never buy another book from Silhouette, the two free books and gifts are mine to keep forever.

225 SDN EEXJ   326 SDN EEXU

Name	(PLEASE PRINT)
Address	Apt.
City	State/Prov.	Zip/Postal Code

Signature (if under 18, a parent or guardian must sign)

Mail to the **Silhouette Reader Service™:**
IN U.S.A.: P.O. Box 1867, Buffalo, NY 14240-1867
IN CANADA: P.O. Box 609, Fort Erie, Ontario L2A 5X3

Not valid to current Silhouette Desire subscribers.

Want to try two free books from another line?
Call 1-800-873-8635 or visit www.morefreebooks.com.

* Terms and prices subject to change without notice. NY residents add applicable sales tax. Canadian residents will be charged applicable provincial taxes and GST. This offer is limited to one order per household. All orders subject to approval. Credit or debit balances in a customer's account(s) may be offset by any other outstanding balance owed by or to the customer. Please allow 4 to 6 weeks for delivery.

Your Privacy: Silhouette is committed to protecting your privacy. Our Privacy Policy is available online at www.eHarlequin.com or upon request from the Reader Service. From time to time we make our lists of customers available to reputable firms who may have a product or service of interest to you. If you would prefer we not share your name and address, please check here. ☐

SDES0ʹ

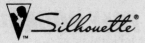

TV journalist Charlie McNally is about
to snag the scoop of a lifetime—proving a
confessed murderer's innocence. Through
all this Charlie has to juggle the needs of
her professor boyfriend and his little girl,
face time with her pushy mom who just
blew into town—and face a deadly
confrontation with the real killer....

Look for

Face Time

by

Hank
Phillippi Ryan

Emmy® Award-winning
television reporter

Available October
wherever you buy books.

ATHENA FORCE

Heart-pounding romance and thrilling adventure.

A deadly masquerade

As an undercover asset for the FBI, mafia princess Sasha Bracciali can deceive and improvise at a moment's notice. But when she's cut off from everything she knows, including her FBI-agent lover, Sasha realizes her deceptions have masked a painful truth: she doesn't know whom to trust. If she doesn't figure it out quickly, her most ambitious charade will also be her last.

Look for

CHARADE
by *Kate Donovan*

Available in October wherever you buy books.

COMING NEXT MONTH